I0690196

THEY LIVED EVER AFTER

a novel by

Barbara J. Olexer

Joyous Publishing
Milwaukie, Oregon, U.S.A.

Cover photo: The Phantom Ship, Crater Lake,
Oregon, courtesy National Park Service

Library of Congress Control Number
2002093750

ISBN 0-9722740-0-6

Joyous Publishing
10675 SE 59th Avenue
Milwaukie, Oregon 97222
SAN 254-8518
joyouspub@comcast.net
www.joyouspub.com

Printed in the USA

by Barbara J. Olexer

NONFICTION

Presidential Education: Prelude to Power
The Enslavement of the American Indian
in Colonial Times
Murder of a Soul: The Story of
Captain Jack (screen biography)
What Astrology Means to You: A Handbook of
Astrological Terms, Glyphs, and Applications

FICTION

They Lived Ever After
Death Takes a Flyer
Murder by Accident
If You Can't Trust Your Uncle Sam
Father to the Man
Fossil Rocks
Criminal Justice
Life Is for Damn Ever

This book is dedicated to my children,
Bill, Laurel, and Bryan; to my parents
and grandparents; and all those with whom
I have adventured across the millennia.

Contents

Prologue

1

The row of ornamental orange trees around the parking lot shimmied as the heat rose from the blacktop. It was early evening and only a few cars remained in the lot, those belonging to the owners of the small businesses contained in the row of upscale shops. Business was good in Phoenix, the snowbirds from up north were beginning to flock in for the winter and the local free-spenders were busy, as well.

Two women came out of a shop that specialized in custom designed women's wear. Genevieve Macklin was fortyish, small and dainty, with dark brown hair and dark brown eyes that could flash fire of either passion or rage. Starla Mayhew was thirty-one, a Nordic blond so striking in looks that few people bothered to consider whether she was beautiful. She was tall and willowy, with a perfect complexion.

As Genevieve locked the shop door, Starla crossed to a blue sports car that was parked so the afternoon sun would cast the shade of the orange trees on it. She unlocked the trunk and stowed her portfolio inside, then slid under the wheel and started the motor. Genevieve got in beside her.

"All the same," Genevieve said, continuing a conversation they'd begun inside, "if Mrs. Edwards would lose ten or fifteen pounds, she'd be easier to fit."

"Yes," said Starla, "but not as interesting. She's not really fat, just well padded."

She backed the car around and hesitated only momentarily before plunging into the tail end of the rush hour traffic.

"She wants all the styles she shouldn't wear, too," went on Genevieve.

"Quit complaining," Starla laughed. "If she was easy to please, she'd go to a department store. We get the big bucks for solving problems for women like Mrs. Edwards."

"I'm glad you're feeling like Pollyanna today, since you're the one who's going to have to do the designing."

Starla wasn't the least bit daunted by the prospect of designing seven new outfits for Mrs. Edwards. Although she was fashionably thin herself, she had designed and crafted many garments of many types for plumper figures. The dynamics were different for different figure types but there were lines to fit and flatter almost any woman. She smiled at Genevieve.

"That's right," she said. "Today I'm glad, glad, glad. And it's the best of all possible worlds."

Genevieve spoke with a trace of sourness, "In fact, it's the maddest, merriest day of all the glad new year."

"That's right."

"I'm 'glad' to hear it, Starla. I was beginning to think you and Pat were headed for the rocks."

"Maybe. Sometimes I'm afraid of that, too." Starla's gaiety overlaid a strand of somberness. "But not today. Today my Patrick can do no wrong. Unless, of course, he stands me up. But he won't, not tonight."

"Stop me if I'm out of line, but I don't understand. I've known you and Pat for six or seven years – since before you and I formed this partnership – and you're obviously in love. It's practically indecent how much you love each other. But you fight all the damn time."

Starla pulled into the parking lot of an automobile dealership and stopped near the door to the service department.

"I know," she said. "I don't understand it, either. It's heaven when he's not weirded out."

"But, being a man…"

Starla interrupted. "Yeah, being a man, he's weirded out pretty much all the time."

4

They both laughed. Genevieve looked at the big plate glass window of the dealership.

"I hope my car is ready," she said. "If it's not, those clowns are going to wish they'd taken up nuclear thermodynamics instead of auto mechanics."

"No, they'll think you did," Starla grinned. "Maybe I'd better wait and see if they need protection."

"It's all right. If the car isn't ready, I'll make them take me home. It's only a mile or two and I guarantee they'll be delighted to take me anywhere I want to go."

Genevieve got out of the car.

"Okay," Starla said. "See you Monday."

"Okay. Happy weekend."

"You, too."

Starla drove away, forgetting all about her partner before she'd gone a block. Meeting her adorable and exceedingly handsome husband for dinner was still exciting after six years of marriage.

Patrick Mayhew was a partner in the fashionable and highly successful architectural firm of Marcus, Phelan, and Mayhew. Pat was in his early thirties – square-jawed and muscular. He was engrossed in sketching the side elevation of a home that was mostly glass when Marjorie Phelan invaded his office. Marjorie was a few years older than he, attractive and exquisitely groomed.

"Hi, Pat," she said. "Am I interrupting something brilliant and fragile?"

"Not at all. Come in. You're just the woman I wanted to see."

He set his pencil down and turned on his stool to face her. Marjorie perched on his desk, winced, reached behind her and moved a small cluster of amethyst crystals away from her backside.

"And now your prayer's been answered. Here I am."

"I need your advice."

She dropped her bantering manner. "What is it, Pat? Is it Starla?"

"Not exactly. No, it's more me than Starla. Marjorie, I don't know what's happening to my marriage."

"I don't know why you're asking me. I'm a three-time loser."

"It's because you have been married three times. You must know something about what makes a marriage go sour."

"Yes. I know a little about it. But I'm only going to give you one piece of advice. See a shrink. In the trite phrase, seek professional help."

"I've thought about it," Pat confessed. He hesitated. "Do you know of a good one?"

"As it happens, I do. Her name is Parker. She's just down the street. She put Jimmy – you remember my second husband, don't you? James F. Carlisle? Anyway, Dr. Parker put him back together after I drove him crazy."

"She?"

"Oh, come on, don't go all macho on me at this point. She's good and she can help you keep it together with Starla. Psychology isn't practiced with the sex organs, you know."

"All right, all right. Thanks. Now, what can I do for you?"

"I want the client specs for the Murchison home. Have you got them?"

"Yes, I think so." Pat crossed to a table and scrabbled through some papers. "Here they are."

He handed Marjorie a sheaf of papers. She took them and slid off the desk.

"Thanks." At the door she turned and remarked, "I thought you had a dinner date."

"Is it that late?" Pat looked at his watch. "I'd better get going."

He put his jacket on, stuffed some papers in his briefcase, and followed Marjorie out of the room.

It was dusk as Starla pulled into the parking lot at the gourmet Mexican restaurant. She carefully locked the car and affixed the anti-theft device to the steering wheel.

The restaurant was crowded but the headwaiter greeted her promptly.

"Good evening, Mrs. Mayhew. Your husband has not yet arrived but your table is ready."

"Thanks, Dionisio."

She followed him through the big room and across a small dining room to a table in a quiet corner. She tipped him and sat down in the chair he held for her.

"Thank you, señora. Enjoy your dinner."

Starla smiled at him. "Yes, I will."

It was fully dark when Pat pulled his three-quarter ton four-wheel-drive pickup into the parking lot at the restaurant. He jumped out, stuffed the keys into his pocket, and hurried inside. There was a line of customers waiting for tables and they eyed Pat resentfully as he went directly to the headwaiter's tall desk and Dionisio immediately ushered him into the dining room. Pat stopped at the door to a second room.

"Okay, Dionisio, I see her. Thanks." Pat tipped him.

"Thank you, Mr. Mayhew." Dionisio smiled and turned back into the main dining room, as Pat crossed to Starla.

She had an empty Margarita glass in front of her and the waitress was serving another.

Pat pulled out a chair. "Bring me one of those, will you, Lucille?"

The waitress smiled at him as he sat down. "Sure thing, Mr. Mayhew. How y'all doin' this evening?"

"Fine, thanks."

Lucille went to fetch his drink and Pat took Starla's hand in his.

"How y'all?" he asked, smiling into her eyes.

"I'm fine," she answered, letting him see her gladness.

Pat leaned over and kissed her.

"I was beginning to think you were going to stand me up," Starla remarked.

"Not a chance," he said, relaxing back against the cushions. "Ah, two whole days all to ourselves."

Lucille brought the drink and handed them menus.

"Thanks," Starla said. She put her menu on the table and turned to Pat, as Lucille moved away. "You really aren't going to work this weekend?"

"I'm not going to the office. I might do a little at home. There's a real teaser of a restoration project I'd like to play with."

"A fun project? Restoring what?"

"It's an old adobe out in the desert toward Tucson. In the Dragoons. It was originally a ranch

9

house. You know, the foot-thick walls and built around a patio."

"And some Yankee built an atrocious frame house and turned the adobe into a barn."

"You got it."

Lucille came back, her pad and pencil at the ready. "Y'all ready to order now?"

"I'll have the number three chile relleno," Starla said. "And bring us a carafe of the red house wine."

"Bring me whatever the chef says is best tonight." Lucille grinned at Pat. "Yes, sir. I believe he's got some kind of concoction with some of them peppers you got to peel under water, 'less you want to blister your eyeballs."

"Sounds wonderful." Pat grinned back at her.

Lucille moved away, chuckling softly and shaking her head.

"Someday you're going to get something so hot you'll burn your tongue right off," Starla warned him.

"Nah. Hot chilies and I get along just fine."

"Tell me some more about your old adobe; it sounds like an exciting project."

"It is. The trick is going to be in keeping the authenticity but incorporating all the modern conveniences. The kitchen and bathrooms won't be so hard because everyone expects them to be updated. But the other rooms will have to be comfortable without looking modern."

"Yes. It won't be easy. Who is going to do the interior design?"

"There's a little firm in Denver. Loveness and Son. They've done some fine Victorians and I think they might be right for this."

"Victorian style is pretty far from Spanish Colonial."

"I know. But they have a real feel for the historicity – they really care about getting things right."

Pat and Starla talked through their meal, sipping the wine, enjoying being together. Pat walked with her to her car and they found themselves in a close embrace, kissing passionately.

"I wish we didn't have two cars tonight," murmured Pat.

"Me, too. Come on, let's hurry home."

Starla turned in his arms and opened the car door. Pat nuzzled her ear.

"We could leave your rig and pick it up tomorrow," she suggested.

"I'm hoping we won't have to come into town at all tomorrow," he said.

Starla turned and they kissed again. Finally Pat let her go and stepped back.

"I'll see you in ten minutes," Starla said.

"Twelve, you impetuous thing."

Starla grinned at him. "Ten."

She unlocked the anti-theft device and started the car. She squealed her tires going out of the parking lot. Pat watched her fondly, shaking his head, as he went to his pickup and climbed in.

Pat had designed their home and together they had chosen the furnishings and color schemes. It was ultra-modern, built of stone and glass, and situated out in the desert with no other homes in sight, although the lights of Phoenix formed a backdrop. Starla pulled into the driveway, admiring the house as her car lights swept across the front of it. She loved the house and the home that she and Pat had made of it.

Inside, Starla took her portfolio to the studio and leaned it against her slant board. Half the studio was devoted to her work and half to Pat's. It was cleverly designed so that it looked like two studios and neither the fashion designs nor the architectural designs were incongruous. A wall of glass gave the room an abundance of clear northern light.

Starla went quickly into the bedroom and flipped the light switch. Another wall of glass, this time facing south, opened onto the patio and swimming pool. She pressed the switch to activate the outside lights. Wanting to greet Pat wearing her new swimsuit, Starla changed rapidly. She glanced at the clock and was puzzled that twenty minutes had gone by since she left the restaurant parking lot. Surely Pat ought to be home by now. Maybe, she thought, he'd stopped to pick up a snack for later. Taking a towel, she went out to the pool, checked for swimming rattlers, and, seeing none, dove in. She swam several laps, enjoying the water and the night.

When Pat got home about ten minutes later, Starla was swimming laps underwater. He called her name as he closed the front door and again as he came into the bedroom. He saw her clothes where she'd tossed them onto a chair, glanced into the bathroom, and then went out to the patio. When he saw Starla at the bottom of the pool, he didn't even stop to kick off his shoes, he simply dove and pulled her to the surface, towing her toward the shallow end. Starla struggled, not knowing who or what had grasped her. When they got to the shallow end, Pat loosened his hold. Starla stood up, gasping for air. Pat also stood up and moved to enfold her in his arms. The look on her face stopped him.

"Pat," she sputtered, "what the hell are you doing?"

"My God. I couldn't find you in the house and

when I looked out here, you were at the bottom of the pool."

Starla was shaken up from being suddenly manhandled and to discover it was her own husband who did it because he thought she was incompetent was irritating, to say the least. She stalked up the steps and out of the pool. She wrapped her towel around herself. Pat hoisted himself out of the pool and sat on the end of a chaise to pull his shoes off.

"What did you think?" Starla asked. "That I'd drowned myself?"

"No, of course not. But I've asked you again and again not to swim alone. It's dangerous."

Starla laughed, trying to keep her temper. "I'm all right. I'm a good swimmer. You nearly gave me a heart attack, grabbing me like that."

"How was I to know you were all right? You didn't answer when I called."

"I was swimming underwater," she said.

"I don't see why, just for once, you couldn't do what I ask."

Starla said, "Well, I thought you'd be home in a few minutes. I didn't expect to be swimming alone, actually."

Pat had been badly frightened and reaction took the form of bad temper. "I had a flat tire and it took a little while to change it." He stood up, the

14

sodden shoes in his hand. "Listen, Starla, don't be so illogical. When you get into the pool when there's no one else home, that's swimming alone. Now, look, you've ruined these pants and shoes."

"I've ruined them! And you call me illogical. I'm not the idiot who jumped into the pool with all my clothes on."

"Fine, now I'm an idiot. Next time, I'll let you drown."

"I wasn't drowning. I was fine. I'm still fine."

"There's no need to blow your stack. I was just trying to keep you safe."

Starla lost her temper. "Then I'd think you'd be happy that I am safe instead of standing there, looking ridiculous, having a tantrum."

"Damn," said Pat as his wife stormed into the house and slammed the bathroom door behind her. "Damn, damn, damn."

Starla quickly stripped off her wet bathing suit, dried herself and slipped on a robe. She pulled a paper cup from the dispenser and filled it. Setting the water on the vanity top, she reached into the linen closet and took a packet of birth control pills from under a stack of towels. She was just taking one out of the packet when Pat opened the door and came in.

"May I come in?" he asked, politely and apologetically. "I need a towel." He saw the pills and snatched the packet from her. "Birth control pills?"

"Damn you," Starla raged. "Can't I have even a second's privacy?"

"I thought we'd decided to have a baby."

"I'm not ready yet. I've told you and told you, I'm not ready to be a mother yet."

"Then why did you agree with me that it's time to start a family?"

"To shut you up."

Pat looked stricken, handed her the pills, and went into the bedroom. Starla threw the pills down and ran after him.

"Pat. Pat."

Pat stripped off his wet clothes and wrapped himself in a robe, ignoring his wife.

"Pat, I'm sorry. I didn't mean that."

Pat looked at her then. "I think you did." His voice was cold. "I think you were startled into telling the truth for once."

Starla's eyes were full of pleas. "Listen to me, Pat. Please. I know I told you it would be nice to have a baby. And I told you I had quit taking the birth control pills. But it was only because you talked about having a baby so much and I want to have one, too. But not yet."

"You've been saying that for the last four and a half years. First you wanted to wait until you got

16

established in your career. Then it was because you wanted to get a partnership first. Then it was because it wouldn't be fair to Genevieve to take a leave of absence just then. Can you blame me for thinking you don't really want a baby? You've lied to me and tricked me again and again and I'm sick of it."

"I know. I know it was wrong. But, please, Pat, try to see it from my point of view. In another six months I'll be ready. I just need that much longer to be so well established that I can do most of my work at home and have time for you and the baby, too."

"Your work. That's all you really care about. Is that why you married me? To have a meal ticket while you get your career established?"

Starla put her hand on his arm but he shook it off. She began to cry.

"Don't say things like that. I married you because I love you. You know I love you."

"I used to think so. Now, I don't know. Maybe it would be better if we split up."

"No. Don't say that, Pat. I'd die if you ever left me."

"Would you?"

Seeing her real distress, Pat was moved to let his anger go. After all, she was the woman of his choice, the wife whom he loved with all his heart.

He took her in his arms and she held him tightly.

She took a deep, shuddering breath. "I couldn't live without you. Don't you know that?"

"I know I wouldn't want to even try to live without you."

"I love you so much. I hate these fights we get into."

"So do I. Let's make a pact never to fight again."

"Never again." Starla smiled up at him.

"I love you, Starla. You're the reason I'm alive. You're my heart."

Saturday morning Pat and Starla swam and lazed in the sun, enjoying the serenity after the storms of the night before. At length they realized they were hungry and went inside to dress and fix brunch. Pat was chopping radicchio with a knife that had a two-inch blade while Starla compounded the salad dressing. The spice rack was in front of Pat.

"Hand me the tarragon, will you?" Starla asked.

Pat found the right jar and handed it to her. "Your tarragon, ma'am."

"Thank you, sir." She added the tarragon to her dressing. "Haven't you finished your chopping yet?"

"I could chop a lot more efficiently if I had a

knife with a longer blade."

Starla frowned. "I think that's the longest one we have."

"I know it is," Pat confirmed, making a face at the blade. "It's enough to suicide one's self, that we have no decent knives."

Starla looked up just in time to see Pat reverse the knife and stab his chest with the handle. She burst into tears.

"Only," continued Pat, not seeing that she was crying, "we don't have a blade long enough for suicide."

"How could you?" Starla shrieked.

She rushed out of the room. Pat was horrified at what he'd done. Knowing her deep-seated phobia about knives, he should never have said anything about death in connection with one and he should certainly never have pretended to stab himself in front of her. Angry with himself and irritated with Starla, he slashed at the head of radicchio. He stuck the knife in the cutting board and went out onto the patio.

Starla had gone straight to their bedroom and was packing. Upset as she was, she was too fond of clothes to wad them up any old way; she folded them carefully and laid them gently in the suitcase. Pat strode up and down by the pool, trying to calm down and think of what to say to

Starla to heal this new breach. At length he opened the glass door and went into the bedroom.

"I'm sorry, Starla. I should have remembered your phobia about knives and suicide. It was a stupid joke." His eyes made the adjustment from the bright outside sunshine to the dimmer light inside and he saw what Starla was doing. "Why are you packing?"

"I'm leaving, Pat. I just can't take any more. You're insensitive to the point of cruelty."

"I'm cruel? You lie to me, trick me, about an issue as important as having a child; and I make a silly joke. But I'm the one who's cruel. I'm insensitive."

"I never claimed to be perfect. If you wanted a perfect wife, you should have married that little French hellcat you were living with when we met. She would have had four or five kids by now. She'd probably be the big fat president of the P.T.A. But she would be a wonderful wife, not like me, the liar and cheat."

"What do you want from me? I've given you everything I have. If it's not enough, I'm sorry. I'm drained, exhausted."

"I don't want anything from you but a divorce."

Pat stared at her for a moment, then turned and went into the hall. In a minute, Starla heard his pickup start. She picked up a lead crystal potpourri jar and smashed it against the wall. She threw herself on the bed, sobbing with frustration and heartache.

Pat drove out into the desert, as far away from human habitations as he could conveniently get. He took a .22 pistol from the jockey box and loaded it. He sat there for a long time, the gun in his hand, thinking what a mess life was. He thought about cleaning it up by putting a bullet in his brain but he wasn't seriously suicidal. In spite of his grief, life was far too interesting to leave it. He hung the blanket-sided water canteen from an arm of a nearby saguaro cactus and gave it a sideways push. Standing back a respectable distance, he fired at the canteen. Water spurted from the bullet holes, falling meaninglessly on the desert floor. Pat emptied the casings from the pistol and put it back in the jockey box. He drove home in a mixed mood of amusement at himself and hope that he and Starla could get things straightened out between them.

Starla's car was not in the driveway. He went to the kitchen and found everything had been cleaned up and put away. He got a bottle of wine out of the refrigerator, drew the cork, and took it and a glass to the studio. Starla's portfolio was gone, along with many of her tools. In the

21

bedroom, the smashed potpourri jar had been picked up. The closet showed a big gap and her cosmetics were gone from the bathroom.

Pat took his wine out to the patio and sat on a chaise longue. At midnight he was still there, the wine untasted. Later, when he thought about why he hadn't drunk the wine, he found it was because he wanted to solve the problem instead of numbing himself to it. Why, loving Starla as deeply and completely as he did, was he constantly angry with her? It made no sense.

Starla was just as deeply and completely in love with Pat as he with her. She sat in a motel room and thought about their relationship. It hurt her terribly to be apart from him, to know that she was hurting him. But she couldn't face their constant battles any longer. She decided that the best thing for both of them would be to get a divorce and forget trying to make a life together.

Several weeks after Starla moved out of the house and into an apartment in Scottsdale, she hired a lawyer who duly notified Pat of her decision. She had steadfastly refused to see or speak to Pat so he called Genevieve and invited her to dinner. They met at a downtown restaurant and Genevieve gave him a hug. Pat waited until after they'd eaten to broach the subject that they both knew was the reason for his invitation.

"I know you and Starla have discussed this thing. She isn't really going through with it, is she?"

"I don't know, Pat. She seems adamant."

"She can't be. Look, Genevieve, you're her partner and her best friend. You can talk her into seeing me. I can't go on like this much longer. I can't work, I can't sleep, I don't eat. I can't even drink."

"You certainly look like hell," Genevieve concurred.

"I got a letter from her lawyer yesterday. He wants to talk to my lawyer, to negotiate the divorce settlement. I don't have a lawyer. I don't want one."

"I think you'd better get one. Before the court makes the settlement for you."

"I don't give a single damn about the settlement. It's Starla I care about. I've been seeing a shrink twice a week ever since she left me. Tell her that. Tell her I'm doing everything I can to get it together for her, if she'll just wait a bit."

"I don't know, Pat. She's hurt and she's scared. She's afraid to risk it with you again."

"I know. I know I made a mess of it. But she can't throw it all away. Listen, Genevieve, Starla loves me. I know she does. She couldn't forget me any more than I could forget her. We belong together."

"She knows that. It isn't that she wants a divorce, I don't think. I think she's afraid of how you hurt each other when you're together. She's scared that it'll never get better."

"Okay, I understand that. That's why I'm seeing the shrink. Just get her to put the lawyer on hold for a little while. Get her to talk to me when I call."

"I don't know if I can. But I'll do my best."

"Thank you. Thanks, Genevieve."

Part I

His Loving Daughter

Pat had been seeing Dr. Parker for a couple of months and his originally high hopes were beginning to flag. He had cleared up some old childhood stuff but he didn't feel he had made any real progress in solving his marital problems. Today he intended to ask her point blank if there wasn't some other way to tackle his troubles.

Dr. Parker opened her office door and called him in right on time. He sat in the chair at the end of her desk and she sat facing him. She was a beautifully elegant woman. Her skin was so dark as to be almost black and she was dressed in a skirted suit that simply shouted professional confidence.

"How are you, Pat?" she asked.

"About the same. Everything's just the same."

"The reconciliation with Starla hasn't worked out?"

"I couldn't even talk her into having dinner with me, much less into a reconciliation. She's still living in the apartment and I'm living in the house."

"I've given your case a lot of thought. Since

none of the therapies we've tried have done much good, I would like to try regression therapy."

"Regression?"

"We've talked about religion and I'm aware that you believe it's merely superstition." Dr. Parker leaned forward earnestly. "But I think your problems may stem from previous lifetimes."

"Reincarnation? Come on, Doc. In the first place, I don't think you can hypnotize me and in the second place, I don't believe in that kind of crap."

"I can't hypnotize you if you aren't willing. I wouldn't even try. As for your other objections, what have you got to lose by trying it?"

Pat moved restlessly. "Nothing I guess."

"We here in the western hemisphere are about the only people on Earth who don't profess belief in reincarnation. I can treat you but I'll be doing a lot of guesswork and it'll take a long time. I'd rather have your full cooperation and work on a factual basis."

"I guess we could try. I'm not doing so hot on my own. But if it doesn't work, we'll just forget about it. Right?"

Dr. Parker smiled. "Right."

"What do we have to do? Do I stare at a pocket watch or what?"

"Let's go into the other room; there's a comfortable chair there and it's quieter."

Pat settled into the recliner somewhat uneasily while Dr. Parker sat in a straight chair beside him. She held a pad and pencil but on a small table to her left was a sound-activated tape recorder. She took Pat through the long, elaborate preliminaries and finally he relaxed into a deep hypnotic trance.

"I want you to remember the first time you knew Starla," Dr. Parker said, her voice calm and low-pitched. "Go back to the first lifetime in which you were together. Tell me what you see."

Pat's voice was matter-of-fact. "I'm sitting on a sort of patio of dressed stone. There's a pool in the center and a garden around me. It's very colorful and lovely."

"Is there anyone else there with you?"

"Yes. There's a gardener clipping some shrubs."

"Where is this house? Do you know the name of the country?"

"Atlantis."

"And the time?"

"There's no way to tell you that. We don't count time the same as you."

"Is it before the land was broken up into islands?"

"Yes. It's all one large land mass. There are enormous beasts that are very bothersome. They destroy our crops and homes."

"How are you dressed?"

"In a kind of robe with sandals." Pat's voice held a little surprise at his costume.

"Are you a man or a woman?"

Pat laughed contemptuously. "A man, of course."

"How old are you?"

"Aren't you listening?" Pat demanded impatiently. "We don't count time the same as you."

"How old do you look?"

"In the thirties. But Atlanteans live to great ages and never look more than that. I'm much older than thirty."

"Where's Starla?"

"In the house. I've asked her to bring a certain scroll to me."

"Is she your wife?"

"She is my daughter. My youngest daughter and my favorite child."

Pat described scene after scene. He seemed to be omniscient as he gave details that he hadn't actually seen and he described himself as if he were describing another entity.

In a deciduous forest, some distance from any

habitation, a duckbilled hadrosaur browsed on the leaves. The dinosaur was about twenty feet long, with a heavy body and a long neck. There were long streamers of a rough fabric hanging from some of the limbs and this made a loud rustling noise when the hadrosaur brushed against it. He was uneasy at the noise but continued to browse.

The hadrosaur failed to see a lookout that was posted on a platform atop the long stone wall that divided the forest from cultivated fields. The lookout was a winged man, a Thing. There was a time when it was possible for all living things to interbreed and this resulted in Things – part human, part animal. Some even had plant parts such as bark and leaves. But most of the Things were humans that were part animal and were of low intelligence.

The winged man, named Stren, was clad only in a loincloth. He watched the forest attentively. When he heard the fabric rustling, he turned toward it and caught a glimpse of the hadrosaur. He immediately spread his wings and flew across the fields to give the alarm.

Simahja – as Pat was known in the Atlantean incarnation – was a handsome man with red skin and black hair that was waxed and arranged in braided coils. His robe was long and loose and decorated with geometric designs. He was sitting on the patio, reading a scroll with deep concentration.

The house was large, built of dressed stone arranged in patterns of red, white, and black. The garden around the patio was beautiful, lush and blooming. Some of the blossoms were two feet in diameter. The patio was paved in the same geometric motif as the house itself and there was a large pool at one end. A couple of lambs, shorn in complicated designs, frisked about the patio. Kawb, a Thing who was half man, half horse, was clipping the shrubbery at the far end of the pool.

Brelwys – as Starla was known – came out of the house carrying a scroll. She, too, was red-skinned and black-haired. She had an elaborate coiffure, waxed and bedecked with golden ornaments set with jewels. She was near the end of her pregnancy and wore a long white robe trimmed with black bands at the throat and hem. She took the scroll to Simahja and handed it to him.

"Here it is, Father, the latest of Mabon's writings."

Simahja smiled up at her. "Is this the one that gives the breeding habits of the ancients?"

"Yes, in this he explains how it came about that we have such anomalies as centaurs, winged men, and so on."

"Good," said Simahja. "That's the one I need. Thank you, Brelwys."

As Simahja unrolled the scroll, the sound of wingbeats caused him and Brelwys to look up. Stren, the winged man from the forest lookout, alighted in the garden. Simahja put the scroll down and went to him.

"What is it?" Simahja demanded. "You've seen one of the great beasts?"

"Yes, Master, along the northwest wall."

"What kind?"

"Big," said Stren, his awe reflected in his face. "Very, very big."

"A meat-eater?"

"No, Master. It was eating leaves."

Simahja turned to the gardener. "Kawb."

The gardener trotted over to Simahja. "Yes, Master?"

"Send someone to alert Xadir to take the logging crew out to the northwest sector, to the wall. And get my basket ready."

"Yes, Master."

"Prepare mine, also," ordered Brelwys.

Simahja gave her a disapproving look but said nothing. Kawb hurried to do as he'd been told. Simahja spoke to Stren.

"You stay and guide us to the place."

"Yes, Master."

Kawb trotted down the path and around the house. Stren followed at a slower pace. Simahja and Brelwys went into the house.

Kawb had prepared the baskets, which were propelled by crystals that were exposed to the sun. The baskets were not operated mechanically but rather by thought; as the occupant willed, so the basket moved. The baskets stood in the workyard of the plantation – sheds and barns stood in a neat square around the perimeter on three sides, with the house and garden forming the fourth, separated by a high hedge from the work buildings.

Kawb, Stren, and several other Things stood near the baskets. Simahja, wearing a kilt, much like the ones worn by ancient Egyptian men, and Brelwys, dressed in a short robe, crossed the yard to the baskets.

"Get my harpoon," Simahja barked at one of the Things, who scurried off obediently.

"Get mine, too," Brelwys called after him.

Simahja shot her a look of exasperation then turned to Kawb.

"Have you sent someone to tell Xadir and the crew to go out to the northwest wall?"

"Yes, Master."

The Thing returned with the harpoons and handed one to Simahja and the other to Brelwys.

Simahja signaled for Stren to lead the way. Stren spread his wings and lifted seemingly effortlessly into the air. Simahja and Brelwys climbed into their baskets and were almost instantly airborne. They flew above the forest, silently and swiftly. Stren dipped his right wing to indicate that the place he'd seen the hadrosaur was just ahead. He perched on a tree branch and the two baskets hovered beside him.

"Locate Xadir," Simahja ordered. "Tell him to bring the crew in from that direction." He pointed and brought his arm sweeping around in a wide arc. "Have them fan out across the forest in a semicircle. He will know what that means. Repeat the instructions."

Stren's brows contracted as he concentrated fiercely to repeat what Simahja had said. "Find Xadir. Tell him to bring the crew in from there and to fan out in a…"

"Semicircle."

"Fan out in a semicircle," repeated Stren.

"Good. Now go."

"Yes, Master."

Stren soared off his branch and Simahja turned to Brelwys.

"You ought to go back."

"Possibly. But I'm not going to." She smiled sweetly at her father.

"This won't come to anything," he said. "With all the noise that idiot's wings make, the beast has probably taken alarm and fled."

"Look," said Brelwys, pointing, "there's Xadir."

Simahja took his basket a little higher so he could see better.

Xadir was a man with goat's legs. He walked uprightly and his eyes gleamed with intelligence. Five other Things accompanied him, distanced to make a curving line. None of them carried weapons.

Stren flew ahead of them to land again near Simahja and Brelwys.

"Master," Stren said excitedly, "the great beast is between you and Xadir. It is still eating leaves."

"That's fine, Stren." Simahja looked at Brelwys, "Come along, if you're coming."

Keeping a good distance between them, Simahja and Brelwys guided their baskets over the forest toward Xadir and the other Things. Brelwys spotted the hadrosaur first. It was browsing but uneasy and restless. It straightened its long neck and looked around alertly. Brelwys shouted to her father and pointed at the hadrosaur. Simahja saw it and they skimmed over the treetops toward it. The beast saw them and bellowed, crashing through the woods, toward the thin line of Things.

Simahja maneuvered his basket to striking distance and threw the harpoon, aiming for the great blood vessels in the neck. The harpoon struck the hadrosaur a glancing blow. The beast continued to bellow and flailed the air with its forelegs as its long tail whipped back and forth. As Simahja hauled his harpoon back into the basket, Brelwys threw hers. It lodged in the beast's neck muscles but missed the great blood vessels. She pulled her harpoon free and was aiming for another blow when Simahja threw his again. That time it pierced the animal's throat but left the arteries intact. The bellowing stopped and the beast took long gasping breaths, fighting for air. Simahja jerked his harpoon free but before he could strike again, the hadrosaur began to run.

Simahja shouted a warning. "Xadir! Don't let it get away!"

The Things moved toward the hadrosaur, yelling and waving their arms, trying to frighten it into stopping. But the animal was crazed with pain and fear and ran straight into the Things, who scrambled to get out of the way. Lowf, a Thing with only the skin of a horse to distinguish him from humankind, slipped and fell. The hadrosaur's left foot came smashing down on Lowf's abdomen, crushing him. Lowf screamed and writhed on the ground in agony. The great beast escaped into the dense woods where the baskets couldn't maneuver. Simahja and Brelwys followed above the treetops for a bit but soon realized that pursuit was hopeless.

They turned back toward home but Brelwys noticed the Things gathered around Lowf.

"Look, Father," she called, "one of the Things is hurt."

Simahja was annoyed at not killing the hadrosaur. He looked down at Lowf and took his basket down to hover beside the stricken Thing.

"If you Things had stood your ground," Simahja told them, "we might have killed that beast."

Brelwys looked up from Lowf to Xadir. "How badly is he hurt?"

"Very bad, Mistress."

"How will you get him home so he can be taken care of?"

"I don't know," Xadir answered.

"I'll send out one of the big baskets," said Brelwys.

"That's very kind of you, Mistress," said Xadir. The other Things looked at her gratefully. Lowf moaned and opened his eyes. With difficulty he focused on Brelwys. A sudden movement by Simahja caught his attention and his eyes widened in horror. Brelwys looked over at her father just in time to see him hurl his harpoon at Lowf, hitting him in the heart.

"Father, no," she shrieked, knowing as she did so that it was already too late.

Simahja nodded at Xadir who went to pull the harpoon free.

Brelwys was near tears. "I came to kill one of the great beasts, not one of our own Things."

Simahja spoke to Xadir. "Clean the harpoon off." He turned to his daughter, rather puzzled at her emotion. "There are plenty of Things to work the logging crew. It's no great loss."

Brelwys didn't answer. She had never understood her father's attitude regarding the Things. She elevated her basket and flew back home.

Later, in the dusk, Brelwys joined the children on the patio. She wore a fresh long robe and her hair was arranged in a different, more elaborate style with jewels and ornaments. The two lambs were curled up together in a patch of golden light cast by a torchere. Four children – two girls and two boys between the ages of five and ten – more or less ran wild as they played in and around the pool. Two nursemaid Things watched them. Brelwys sat with a two-year-old girl on her lap, listening to a long and unintelligible story.

Simahja came across the garden to the patio. There had been some matters to attend to on the plantation and he was just then getting back after the hadrosaur hunt. The children saw him and ran to him, calling greetings to their father and grandfather and giving him bits of news. He sat beside Brelwys and the children gathered around him. The little girl slid down from Brelwys' lap and went to Simahja. He picked her up and she cuddled against him.

"Did you kill the great beast, Grandfather?" asked one of the little boys. He frowned at Brelwys in displeasure. "Mother won't tell us."

"What kind of beast was it?" asked the other boy.

"Was it a meat-eater?" one of the little girls asked, avid for gory details.

"No," said Simahja, "it wasn't a meat-eater. And, no, we didn't kill it. We wounded it but the Things let it get away before we could finish it off."

"Tell us what happened, Father," implored the older boy.

Simahja looked around for one of the nursemaids. "Muak, bring something to drink."

"Yes, Master." Muak went into the house.

Simahja glanced around at the children. "You want to hear all about the epic battle with the great beast?"

There was a chorus of assents as the children seated themselves in a semicircle in front of him and Brelwys.

"There wasn't that much to it," Simahja told them. "The Things formed a line on the ground to frighten it into staying there. Brelwys and I attacked from the baskets. We wounded it but it broke out past the Things and got away."

"Where did you wound it?" asked the blood-thirsty little girl.

"Brelwys' harpoon struck it in the neck. Mine struck once in the neck and once in the throat."

One of the boys asked thoughtfully, "Mayn't it died anyway?"

Muak came out of the house carrying a tray with a big silver jug and cups. She poured a cup of fruit juice and handed it to Simahja, who immediately drank it down. She then served Brelwys and the children.

Simahja answered seriously. "It might. Though I don't think it was wounded as badly as that."

"Why not tell them what you did kill?" asked Brelwys.

"Why?" shrugged Simahja. "Lowf was only a Thing."

Muak dropped the jug. The other nursemaid

shot a look of fear at Simahja and hurried to Muak. Simahja ignored them.

"Oh, Lord, I forgot they were here," Brelwys said. "Lowf was Muak's husband."

Simahja laughed shortly. "Her husband? That's a good joke – marriage among the Things." He gave the child on his lap a kiss and set her on the pavement. "I must go and make myself presentable for dinner."

He went into the house and as soon as the door closed behind him, Muak went to Brelwys.

"Please, Mistress. Tell me what has happened. The Master has killed Lowf?"

"I'm sorry, Muak," Brelwys said compassionately. "Lowf was very badly injured in the fight with the great beast. My father killed him to save him further suffering."

"No." Muak's eyes were big with pain. "No, no, no, no."

Brelwys spoke to the other Thing. "Take her out of here. Get her away from the children. And send Farila to me."

"Yes, Mistress."

Weeping hopelessly, Muak allowed herself to be led into the house.

Later that night, after dinner, Brelwys and Simahja sat in the salon. There were no doors between the public rooms, just archways. There was a fireplace in one wall and frescoes decorated the others. The floor was covered with geometric tiles. Cushioned chairs and benches constituted most of the furniture but there were a couple of tables holding scrolls and writing materials. Brelwys was embroidering a tiny garment with stylized flowers; Simahja was rolling up a scroll.

"I suppose as soon as your child is born, you'll be on your way back to Poseidia," he said.

"No, I think I'll have a party."

"For how long?"

"Until harvest, maybe. Then we could go into Poseidia for the festival."

"And who are you thinking of inviting?"

"I think maybe a dozen or so good friends," Brelwys answered.

"Why such a crowd? Why not one or two? We'll have a small hunt."

"Maybe that would be more fun."

"You could invite your child's father."

"Feydja?" she asked, surprised. "I don't know if he hunts."

"Surely he's not as soft as that."

"No, I wouldn't call him soft."

Simahja laughed. "Well, invite him and we'll see if he can change my mind."

"I'll invite him, but not to change your mind about him."

"Please yourself. But be sure you invite Riavay."

"The black woman from Africa? Why? I didn't think you even liked her."

"I don't. But she's very beautiful and I want to see if she and I would produce a beautiful child. And what color it would be."

"Father," demanded Brelwys severely, "do you really think that's a good reason to breed a child? Just to see the color you and a specific woman will produce?"

"Certainly." He went to her and patted her belly fondly, kissing her forehead. "Anyway, you're not in a very strong position to chide me for fecundity. Why did you conceive this one?"

Brelwys laughed. "For no better reason than to see if it would be beautiful, I suppose."

"That's what I thought." Simahja went to the archway that led to the bedrooms. "Good night, Brelwys."

"Good night, Father."

A few days later, Brelwys gave birth to a darling girl child. She was a doting mother and thoroughly enjoyed caring for her new daughter. One bright and sunny day she was sitting in her room in an easy chair, nursing the baby. The baby fell asleep and Brelwys smiled down at her. She stood, intending to put the baby in her crib, but as she crossed the floor, a shaft of sunlight fell across the infant's forehead. Brelwys stopped, horrified at the sight of two tiny horn buds on that otherwise perfect little countenance.

There could be only one meaning to the hornbuds: the baby was a Thing. Brelwys held the child tightly, dismay flooding through her. Angrily, she thought of the child's father. He had deceived her, letting her believe that his bloodlines were as pristine as her own. For there was no doubt in her mind that the tainted blood came from the father's genes and not her own.

Gradually, Brelwys calmed down. She put the baby on the bed, with a pillow on either side of her in case she should roll. She went to the door and called her maid.

"Farila. Farila, come here."

Farila was a female Thing, human except that she had scales instead of skin over most of her body.

"Yes, Mistress?"

"I have made a terrible discovery."

"Mistress, I swear to you that none of us knows how the linens got spoiled. We have all…"

"Shut up. Do you think I care about that now? I have just discovered that my daughter is a Thing."

"Mistress, how terrible." Farila gasped.

"Be quiet. I have no need of your commiseration. You must make some bonnets for her and take very good care that my father does not find out."

"Yes, Mistress."

"You have a daughter, have you not?"

"Yes, Mistress. I have two. The elder one is nearly grown. The younger one is twelve. They are good girls."

"Do they look like you?" Brelwys asked.

"Yes, except that they have scales only on their legs."

"Are they pretty?"

"Yes, Mistress."

"You love them very much, don't you, Farila?"

"Yes, Mistress."

"And I love my daughter very much. But I fear for her if my father should discover these." She picked up the baby and pointed to the horn buds. "If my father finds out about these, I will sell both your daughters to the lowest brothel I can find. Do you understand?"

"Yes, Mistress."

"Very well. Take her now and devise a bonnet while I try to think what can be done."

Farila took the baby from Brelwys.

"Mistress?"

"What is it?"

"The baby's father will be here tomorrow, will he not?"

"Yes," answered Brelwys.

"Then perhaps he could find a way to remove the little horn buds."

"Farila, I have given you an order. Obey me at once."

"Yes, Mistress."

The next morning Brelwys took Feydja, the baby's father, out into the orchard in a flying basket. The fruit was ripe and some Things were on long ladders, picking the golden apricots and rosy peaches. Other Things were on the ground, filling boxes and transporting them to the shed. Brelwys directed the basket to glide slowly between the rows of trees as she and Feydja talked.

"What are you going to do about the child?" Feydja asked.

"I don't know." Brelwys frowned, wondering what she had ever seen in the handsome, shallow man beside her. "I'm afraid my father will kill her if he finds out."

"Or you. It's a real shame. She's a little beauty except for those horn buds."

Brelwys stopped the basket and they sampled some apricots.

"There must be a Thing among your grandparents," she said.

"Just what I was thinking about you. Unless one of your own Things fathered the child."

"I advise you to guard your tongue, Feydja."

He shrugged. "It means little to me. I don't have to explain to my father how I happened to bear a child with horns."

Brelwys started the basket moving again.

"I still haven't found a way to tell my father. Maybe I should just take her to Poseidia. Perhaps he doesn't have to find out."

"Simahja wouldn't actually harm the child?"

"He has absolutely no feeling for the Things. Those tiny little buds would be more than he could accept. I'm afraid of what he might do."

When the basket bearing Brelwys and Feydja landed on the lawn, they saw Riavay inspecting a bed of heart's ease. Riavay, as Dr. Parker was known in the Atlantean incarnation, was in her mid-twenties, a lovely black lady, wearing a long, elegant robe. The flowers were a deep velvety purple with a golden eye in the center. Riavay had picked some and they glowed against the purplish black satin of her skin.

"Good morning, Riavay. You're up and about early," Brelwys greeted her.

"You, too," answered Riavay.

47

"Where's my father?"

"He's out with the logging crew this morning. I'm going to join him. I've never seen a logging operation."

"May I come with you?" Feydja asked.

"If you like," answered Riavay.

Feydja left Brelwys' side and went to Riavay, who smiled to herself.

"Brelwys, would you care to accompany us?" Riavay invited.

"No thanks. I've seen the operation many times. It's not as fascinating as all that. Help yourselves to my basket."

She went toward the house. Feydja and Riavay got into the basket and it lifted off.

A river ran through the forest and it was very beautiful. Feydja and Riavay were skimming over the trees, following the river. The sounds of the logging crew's axes and hand saws were faintly audible. Riavay was looking at the river, Feydja was looking at her.

Springboards, narrow boards driven into the trunk to allow the timber-fallers to stand on them and cut above the thickest part, had been attached to half a dozen trees. Things, including those who acted as beaters the day before, stood on the springboards, chopping industriously. There being no mechanical equipment, teams of oxen dragged the logs over a skid road to be rolled into the river and floated to the sawmill.

Xadir was directing the logging crew as they limbed and bumped the knots from the logs and set the chokers so the oxen could pull the logs away. Simahja and one of the Things were standing on springboards using a felling saw. The tree cracked and creaked and began to tilt. Simahja and the Thing leaped off their springboards, away from the falling trunk.

Simahja yelled, "Timber!"

Feydja and Riavay hovered in their basket near the crew. Simahja watched the tree fall then turned and noticed Riavay. The basket landed and Riavay stepped out. Feydja followed.

"Very impressive," stated Riavay.

Electricity seemed to crackle between her and Simahja. He tossed a nod of civility to Feydja but it was almost as if the younger man wasn't really there.

"Routine," Simahja commented.

"I had no idea you worked as hard as this. Haven't you enough Things to do this sort of work?" Feydja asked condescendingly.

Simahja was amused. "There are plenty of Things. Why? Are you offering your services?"

"Not for this."

"For the hunt maybe," suggested Riavay.

"Most certainly for the hunt," Feydja agreed. "Have you decided on a day for it yet?"

"Tomorrow," answered Simahja. "The great beasts destroyed half the crop of oranges last night." He turned to watch the Things driving the springboards into a tree. "Mhobav," he continued, "who has the plantation to the west, lost most of a new planting of peaches last night, too. So he and his Things will join us."

"It sounds like good sport," Feydja said.

"Good sport? I never kill for sport." Simahja shot the young man a contemptuous glance.

The creaking and groaning of wood rending announced that another tree was about to fall and they all turned to watch it.

"I'll see you this afternoon," Simahja said and went back toward the loggers. Feydja watched Riavay as she watched Simahja.

Later that night Mhobav joined them as they all stood around a map spread out on a table on the patio.

"Does anyone have any idea where the breeding ground is?" Feydja asked.

"I have an idea. I'm not sure it's there but…Well, tomorrow we'll see," answered Mhobav.

"Show us," Brelwys asked.

They all gathered around closer and Mhobav

pointed to the map. "It is always this section of my orchards that are ravaged first. And you, Simahja, yours are always struck from here, are they not?"

"From the northwest, yes," answered Simahja.

"I believe that means the beasts come from here." Mhobav indicated an area on the map. "It isn't all that often that they strike – I think that means they must come from quite a distance. Perhaps even from over the mountains."

"Yes, I see that," said Riavay.

"What's the plan for tomorrow, then?" asked Feydja.

"We have sent contingents of Things to fan out along these lines tonight." Simahja drew his finger along several locations on the map. "At first light tomorrow we'll go up this way as the Things move in toward them, driving the great beasts into the canyons where we can kill them," answered Simahja.

"Then we'll continue up the river, here, until we find the breeding ground," continued Mhobav.

"I gather your wife won't be with us on the hunt," Feydja commented.

"No," said Mhobav, "she has no taste for it."

"How about you, Brelwys?"

Brelwys was surprised at the question. "I'll be there. Of course."

51

"You don't think that until your child is old enough to wean, it would be better to stay with her?" Riavay suggested.

"There is a wet nurse," answered Brelwys shortly, annoyed that the woman dared to insinuate criticism of her. Riavay feigned disgust. "One of the Things will nurse…"

Brelwys interrupted, smiling at Mhobav. "Mhobav, I'll say goodnight. As Riavay has reminded me, my child may be hungry. I'll see you in the morning."

They all bid her goodnight as she went into the house.

"It's time for me to go, also," said Mhobav. "I'll see all of you in the morning."

"Join us for breakfast," invited Simahja.

"All right. Until tomorrow, then."

They nodded goodnights and Mhobav crossed the garden to his basket and flew away. Simahja watched Riavay intently, oblivious to everything and everybody else. Riavay looked at the moonlight reflected in the pool. Feydja looked from one to the other and rose.

"Goodnight," he said.

"Goodnight," answered Riavay.

Feydja went into the house. Riavay walked to the edge of the pool and stood looking down at it. Simahja watched her for a few moments.

"Brelwys tells me you are interested in the heredity of various traits," she commented.

"Genetics," said Simahja.

"What?"

"It's called genetics," said Simahja. "And yes, I'm very interested."

"What aspects interest you most? The traits of the mind or those of the body?"

Simahja ignored her question. "How do you come to be in Atlantis? Your people are African, are they not?"

Riavay nodded. "My father and mother were ambassadors to your court. I grew up in Poseidia. When they were called home, I refused to go. This is my home."

"How many children have you borne?"

"Two, both boys. They are beautiful."

Simahja unfastened his belt and let it fall. He slipped his robe off and tossed it away. He sat on a wide step in the pool, so the water came up to his waist.

"Take off your robe." Simahja's voice was soft but compelling.

Riavay's eyes widened at his directness. He held out his hand to her. Slowly she obeyed and sat on the steps also, leaving a lot of room between herself and Simahja.

"What color are they?" he asked.

"What color are what?

"Your sons. Were they sired by Atlanteans?"

"Yes. Yes, of course," she answered.

"I just wondered what a mixture of red and black would produce. A blend of both colors or does one dominate? Like eyes. Blue-eyed parents can't produce brown-eyed children, you know. Unless one or more grandparents had brown eyes. I just wondered if the same is true of skin."

"They are not red like you," Riavay said. "I suppose you would call the color a blend. Their skin is black but lighter than mine."

Simahja nodded thoughtfully and rubbed the back of his neck. Riavay relaxed and stretched out in the water, knowing that he was watching her. She spoke without looking at him.

"How many children do you have?"

"Nine. Except for my ten-year-old son, Brelwys is the youngest of them."

"Only nine?"

"My wife had difficulty in conceiving."

"I had forgotten that you were married," she said. "You're a widower now?"

"Yes."

Riavay looked up at him and saw that he was still rubbing his neck. He appeared to be looking at something far away but was entirely aware of her smallest movement. She hesitated, then moved to sit on the step beside him. She began to massage his neck and he was quiescent under her touch. She moved up a couple of steps and rubbed his shoulders and back.

"That's wonderful, Riavay. You have the touch of an angel."

"So I've been told."

He turned and put his arms around her. She tipped her head back and he kissed her throat.

The next morning Simahja led the way from the house across the patio to the yard where some Things were ready with the five one-person baskets. Simahja, Brelwys, Mhobav, Riavay, and Feydja were all dressed in short tunics. They got into the baskets and the Things handed them harpoons. After checking the weapons, they flew the baskets over the orchards toward the forest.

They came to a box canyon where two lines of Things, acting as beaters, were noisily converging on the open end, closing it as a line of escape to any hadrosaurs that might be in the canyon.

"Look," Mhobav shouted, "there, beside that pond."

"Hadrosaurs," Feydja cried exultantly.

Two of the great beasts were trotting down a ravine toward the pond in the bottom of the canyon. Simahja quickly gave instructions.

Everyone took their assigned positions. The great beasts thrashed about and their bellowing filled the canyon. The hunters took great care to avoid the lashing tails and the jaws of the hadrosaurs while trying to sever the blood vessels of the neck with their harpoons. At last the beasts were killed and the people were well splashed with blood.

They landed beside the pond.

"A good morning's work," said Mhobav.

"Is there anything to drink?" asked Riavay.

"In my basket," Brelwys said. She got out a clay bottle of wine and passed it around. Simahja walked down to the water and drank. He looked into the calm, clear water and executed a shallow dive. He swam out into the middle of the pond, washed the blood from his skin, then floated on his back with his eyes closed. Riavay swam out to him and the waves she made caused him to open his eyes. She splashed a good deal of water, washing off the blood.

"How do you think the morning's work went?" she asked.

"Excellently," answered Simahja. "We killed the beasts."

"It was my blow that killed the one," Riavay said.

"I saw. You struck it very well."

"Yes, I know," she said complacently.

Brelwys, Feydja, and Mhobav waded into the pond and washed the blood off their faces and arms. After a short respite to eat and rest, the hunters returned to their baskets and, spreading out, flew over the forest, searching for the hadrosaurs' nesting site. Simahja was thinking of giving it up for that day when Brelwys signaled that she'd found something. He flew over to her and they silently circled an opening in the trees. Five hadrosaurs sat on raised mud nests which were just a hadrosaur length apart. Simahja grinned at her and flew back to signal the others.

The hadrosaurs were unaware that the humans were near until the attack began. Mhobav and Brelwys, Riavay and Feydja worked together as teams, while Simahja worked alone. They killed three of the great beasts but two escaped into the forest. Simahja and Mhobav gave chase and killed one more. Feydja and the women landed and set about smashing the eggs in the nests.

One of the supposedly dead hadrosaurs opened her eyes and blinked. Brelwys was standing near her, unaware that she was conscious. The hadrosaur opened her mouth and darted her head at Brelwys' legs. Riavay saw the movement and screamed but it was too late to warn Brelwys. The beast's jaws closed on her legs, crushing them. Brelwys screamed and fell, unconscious from the shock and pain. Simahja and Mhobav returned just in time to see the hadrosaur strike. Simahja rushed to kill the animal, striking many more blows than necessary. He knelt beside his daughter.

"Oh, my God. My dear God. Brelwys."

At home in her room that night Brelwys lay motionless, unconscious. Simahja was sitting beside her bed, agony deeply engraved on his face. He reached out and took her hand; her fingers closed around his. Muak came into the room bringing a small jug and a cup. Simahja spoke to her without taking his eyes from Brelwys.

"Bring the child," he ordered.

"Yes, Master," she murmured, deeply troubled and frightened for Farila had confided Brelwys' secret and her threat.

Muak set the jug and cup on the table and went out. A few moments later she came back in carrying the baby. She gave the child to Simahja and stood beside him uncertainly. He jerked his head at the door in dismissal and she thankfully left, to seek Farila and warn her. Simahja looked down at the infant and smiled. She smiled back at him and he put his finger in her hand; she held on tightly. He kissed her and pushed her cap off her forehead, revealing the miniature horn points.

Incredulously, he touched them, rose and strode from the room.

In the quarters the Things were relaxing around their cook fires; some still eating, others listening to Begili, who was playing a stringed instrument. They stared suspiciously and sullenly at Simahja when he appeared with the baby. Begili stopped playing and Xadir came slowly forward.

"What is it, Master? Is it the Mistress?"

"Your mistress lives yet awhile. Where is the wet nurse?"

Vlesqa came timidly to stand near Xadir.

"Yes, Master?"

Simahja put the baby in her arms. "Take this child. She is one of you. Never let me see her again."

"Oh, Master, I cannot kill her," Vlesqa gasped.

"I said nothing of killing; just keep her out of my sight," answered Simahja.

"Yes, Master."

Simahja turned and went back to the house.

Brelwys was still unconscious in her room the next day, Simahja sitting beside her. At length, her eyes fluttered open and she looked up at her father and smiled before the force of the pain struck and she twisted under its assault. Simahja gave her a drink that contained a strong painkiller and in a few moments she relaxed somewhat.

"My baby?"

"Your baby is being cared for. You mustn't worry. Concentrate on getting well."

"No, Father, I'm not going to get well."

He leaned down and kissed her forehead. "Shhh. Go to sleep," answered Simahja.

Brelwys closed her eyes. Feydja came to stand in the archway, hesitating. Simahja looked at him then back at Brelwys.

"What is it?" he asked.

"How is she?" Feydja replied.

"She's in a great deal of pain."

"Will she recover?"

"I don't think so. The injury seems to have cost her the will to live."

"She would be crippled, of course," Feydja observed.

"By God, I don't see what my daughter saw in you to bear your child. I have no need of your mewling and puking. Go back to Poseidia where you belong," Simahja snarled.

Summoning what dignity he could, Feydja answered. "Yes, that's what I came to tell you. When she wakes, tell her that I'll return if she sends for me. You'll do that?"

"For her sake," answered Simahja.

Later that day Brelwys lay watching Muak, who was clearing up the clutter on the table.

"Where is my baby, Muak?" Brelwys spoke softly, with effort.

Muak dropped a cup and stooped to pick it up.

"Muak, look at me."

Reluctantly, she obeyed. "The little one is in the quarters," she whispered.

"In the quarters?" Brelwys repeated, with a sinking heart, knowing what it meant. Her father had banished her daughter.

"Yes. The Master took her to Vlesqa. He said to keep her away from him because she is a Thing. I could not help it, Mistress. There was nothing I could…"

"Be quiet. Where is Feydja? Is he still here?"

"No, Mistress. The Master sent him away. Back to Poseidia."

"Send for him to come back."

"How can I do that, Mistress?"

"Send Kawb."

"Oh, Mistress, what would the Master do to us if he found out?"

Brelwys beat her fists feebly on the coverlet.

"I must find a way to send for him. I must!"

Simahja came in. "Send for whom? Feydja?"

Muak silently sidled to the door and out of the room.

61

"Yes. Would you, Father? I want to see him once more."

"If you want it so much, of course I'll send for him."

"I do want it. Now?" There was urgency in Brelwys' voice and Simahja responded to it.

"All right, I will send for him now," answered Simahja and went out of the room.

That night, Brelwys was in terrible pain. Muak was wringing her hands in distress.

"Where is my father now?" Brelwys was growing weaker; she knew she had to act at once or she would not be able to act at all.

"He's with the children in the nursery," answered Muak.

"There is only one way I can protect my baby." With many pauses for breath, Brelwys told Muak what she had to do. "Her father will be helpless against mine. And mine will never relent. He has declared her a Thing and he will force her to live as a Thing. But Feydja could take her to Poseidia and the little horns could be removed so she could live her life as a free Atlantean, as she was meant to. I've been lying here thinking of it. It's the only way. You must bring me a knife. A sharp knife. As sharp as a knife can be. Because my strength is nearly gone; I cannot strike more than one blow."

62

"Mistress, please, let me give you a drink of the painkiller. You must be mad with pain, I think."

"I will not take the painkiller. It dulls my mind and I must have all my wits about me. What are you waiting for? Get me the knife while he is with the children," Brelwys ordered.

Muak didn't move.

"My father killed your husband, didn't he? For no good reason. I saw it done. Shall I tell you how his eyes looked when he saw the harpoon in my father's hands aimed at his heart? Bring me the knife."

Muak began to weep but went to do her mistress' bidding. Brelwys also wept, quietly, despairingly. Muak returned in a few minutes, carrying a knife concealed in her robe. She took it out and handed it to Brelwys, who examined it and slipped it under the coverlet. Presently Simahja came in and Muak scuttled away in panic.

"Feydja will be here tomorrow," Simahja told his daughter.

"Thank you, Father." Brelwys tried to smile.

Simahja sat beside the bed and took her hand. He saw that she had been crying and gently wiped away the tears with a soft silken cloth. "I've sent for more physicians, too, Brelwys. Perhaps there's something that can be done for you, after all."

"I'm dying you know. It's no good pretending, is it?" she answered.

Tears streamed down Simahja's face.

"Yes, I know it. It was my carelessness that brought you to this. Your pain is almost more than I can bear."

"Then why in God's name are you creating pain even to my immortal soul by sending my baby away?" cried Brelwys.

"Oh, my dear, surely you know that I cannot do otherwise."

With a sob that he could not conceal, Simahja knelt beside the bed and put his head down on the coverlet. Brelwys stroked his hair.

"Father?"

He lifted his head, now dry-eyed.

She looked deeply into his eyes. "Where is my baby daughter?"

"She's…"

Brelwys interrupted, fearing that he was about to speak a kindly lie. "I need the truth, Father."

"I took her to the wet nurse," he answered.

"To be brought up as a Thing?"

"You knew about the horns."

"There is a new technique that removes such appendages," Brelwys said.

"The taint would remain. She would still be a

Thing."

"No. Those tiny little horns could never make a Thing of my child." Desperation gave Brelwys strength. "You saw for yourself that she's bright and human. She must be given her place here as my daughter."

"She's being cared for."

Brelwys' hand slipped under the coverlet and emerged with the knife gripped tightly. Before he had any inkling of her intent, Brelwys struck, sending the blade deep into Simahja's flesh, penetrating his heart. He stared at her in disbelief and his hands fumbled for the knife handle as he fell forward onto the bed. Tears rained down Brelwys' cheeks as she stroked his hair.

"Oh, God. Oh, God," she cried.

Part II

Black and Beautiful

Pat was lying back in a reclining chair, relaxed in a hypnotic trance. Dr. Parker sat beside him, the tape recorder set, with a pad and pencil for taking notes.

"Tell me about the second life in which you were associated with Starla. What's your name?" she asked.

"Ntare," Pat answered.

"Where are you?"

"On a hilltop."

"What are you doing?"

"Watching. Down the hill some Arabi are going past."

"Arabi?" queried Dr. Parker. "Arabs?"

Pat spoke contemptuously. "Yes. Arabi scum."

"Where is this hilltop located?"

"Burundi. Your name for it is Burundi."

"I don't know where it is. Asia?"

"Africa," said Pat. "At the north end of the lake you call Tanganyika."

"Are you a black man?" asked Dr. Parker.

"Yes, black like you. I hate the Arabi."

"Why do you hate them?"

"They're thieves and murderers. They would enslave our women and piccanins if we allowed them to come on this side of the mountains. They have slaves with them, but not my people. We will set them free anyway. Because we hate the Arabi and they must learn to stay out of our land, on the other side of the mountains."

"How do you count time? Can you tell me when this is?"

Pat was amused. "Not so you could understand. It is before the time of the Nazarene."

"Christ, do you mean?"

"Yes."

"Where is Starla? Is she with you?"

Pat was becoming impatient with Dr. Parker's ignorance. "Starla is not here. And anyway, women stay at home and look after the piccanins. They do not accompany warriors."

"Are you married?"

"Yes, of course. All the men of my people marry when they are of age. My wife's name is Mbonimana. My family paid heavy bridewealth for her."

Dr. Parker had no inkling that she had been the bride in question. She allowed surprise to show in her voice. "You bought her?"

"She is not a slave," Pat said angrily. "She is my wife." He spoke more composedly. "My father chose her for me. When she came to me, her father was bereft and no longer had her work to help the family; so my father paid the brideprice to compensate somewhat for her father's loss." Proudly, Pat went on, "We have two piccanins. Very pretty babies. Soon, I will take another wife."

"Why have you waited to take another wife?"

"I had another but she died in childbirth. One of the piccanins is hers."

"Tell me what you are doing now," Dr. Parker suggested.

It was nearly sunset as Ntare lay on the crest of a hill, in the tall grass, watching. A number of other warriors were similarly concealed. All were dressed in skin kilts with feather headdresses and all were carrying spears. Ntare and a few others had strips of leopard skin in their headdresses, denoting extraordinary bravery and prowess in battle. The warriors were watching a slave-raiding party of Arabs that was riding horseback along a trail below. The slaves, black men, women, and children, were chained together.

The Arabs made camp beside a pond. They picketed the horses out in a meadow and left some of their men as guards. They chained the slaves to acacia trees, but left no one to guard them, knowing the strength of the chains. There was much laughter as the Arabs relaxed around a campfire.

Ntare and the others waited patiently until the Arabs were settled and beginning to get sleepy. At a signal, the warriors left their concealment, moving swiftly and silently toward the Arabs' camp. They erupted into the camp with fierce yells to terrify the enemy and paralyze him with fear. The suddenness of the attack, together with the seemingly large number of warriors and the ferocity with which they used their spears, quickly gave them the victory. The Arabs guarding the horses, seeing the attack on the camp and that their comrades had succumbed, mounted bareback and fled, leaving most of the horses behind.

The warriors did not strip nor mutilate the dead Arabs. They went through the trade goods and other possessions, seeking cloth and iron implements. They broke the Arabs' weapons and set fire to the camp. They broke the slaves' chains, then, forming a line in single file, the warriors trotted along a foot trail up the hill and over it, assisting their few wounded. Ntare looked back as he topped the hill and saw that the slaves had taken up the broken weapons and were hacking at the corpses.

Ntare arrived home two days later, carrying his

spear and a bundle of cloth. He smiled as he approached his round, conical-roofed house and saw his wife, Mbonimana, sitting in the dooryard, weaving a mat. She was dressed in a skin skirt and wore many copper bracelets and a necklace of hammered copper. Her hair was dressed in an elaborate style with many partings and ornaments. Near her a year-old girl and a two-year-old boy were playing, industriously filling a basket with pebbles.

Ntare leaped the vine-covered fence into the midst of his family so suddenly that the two babies began to cry. Mbonimana jumped to her feet.

Ntare laughed. "Did I startle you?"

He leaned his spear against the house and threw the bundle down. He scooped the babies up and they stopped crying to grin at him.

Mbonimana smiled. "You did and no wonder. I thought you were a demented baboon when you first jumped into the yard."

Ntare kissed the babies and tickled them to make them laugh. Mbonimana reached for one of them and he handed her the younger one. Still holding the babies, they embraced and kissed, but not on the lips. Among their people, kissing on the lips was reserved for lovemaking when the procreation of a child was the intent. Greetings over, they sat in front of the house. The babies wiggled to get down and go back to filling the basket. Mbonimana picked up the mat she'd been working on.

"What are you making?" Ntare asked.

"A new love mat," Mbonimana answered, without looking up.

"You missed me," he teased.

"The nights were cold; I missed the warmth of your body."

"Tonight," he said with a grin, "you will be warm enough."

Before Mbonimana could answer, the insistent rhythm of drums, distant but distinct, brought Ntare to his feet.

"Come," he urged excitedly, "the victory dance is about to begin."

"First show me what is in the bundle."

"Some of the strange skin the Arabi use to make robes of. It's pretty and I thought you might like it."

Ntare unrolled the cloth and wrapped it around her. She laughed up at him and he fell to his knees beside her.

"You are so beautiful," he breathed, holding her closely and showering kisses on her face.

"Ntare," she whispered, "the dance."

He unwound the cloth, his mood changing again. "Yes, the dance. Come, be quick."

They each caught up one of the babies and Ntare took his spear. They left the enclosure, walking quickly toward the sound of the drums.

At the ceremonial ground, a crowd was gathered around a leaping bonfire. Everyone was there, warriors, women, old people, and children. The musicians were beating drums and playing marimbas. Everyone watched the warriors as they took their places around the fire and began their victory dance. When that dance was finished, the drums began to play the rhythm for another dance. The women joined the warriors then and the children and even some of the old people danced.

The dancing lasted far into the night. As the children grew sleepy, they were bedded down in the shadows. At last everyone was exhausted with the excitement and the dancing; the drums and marimbas fell silent. Family groups left the ceremonial ground, parents carrying sleeping children, adults moving slowly in their fatigue. Ntare and Mbonimana walked in the moonlight, each carrying a child.

When they reached their home, they put the children to bed, covering them with skin blankets. Ntare took Mbonimana in his arms and kissed her face – her eyes, her cheeks, her chin. She looked deeply into his eyes and kissed his lips.

"Another piccanin?" he queried softly, holding her close to him.

"Many more," she whispered.

Ntare kissed her lips and she clung to him passionately.

The days passed, turning into weeks and months and years. Mbonimana brought forth four more children; Ntare took two more wives and they gave him five more children. In fact, his youngest wife was expecting another at any moment.

One day, as the three wives were tanning some hides in the rear of the yard, Ntare sat in the dooryard. He was playing the marimba as nine of the children danced, laughing happily. The youngest child was but a few months old and slept peacefully at her father's side. Micombero, the eldest son, a fine well-grown ten-year-old, came through the gate and squatted down near his father, waiting to be noticed. He held something in his hand and appeared to be puzzled.

At last, Ntare stopped playing and the children flopped down in the yard to rest. Ntare smiled at Micombero, saw the glint of something in the boy's hand and scowled.

"What is it that you have there?"

Micombero held the object out to his father. It

was a gold nugget, gleaming in the sun.

"I don't know, Father. I found it. Can you tell me what it is?"

"Its name is gold and it's a nasty metal that defiles those who touch it."

Micombero dropped the nugget and looked at his hand in trepidation. "What must I do, Father?"

"Does anyone else know that you have this gold?"

"Some of the other boys were with me when I found it. They took some to show their fathers, also."

Ntare's scowl was very fierce, causing Micombero greater fear. "We didn't know it was wrong," he offered, hoping that would mitigate the offense.

"The fault is not yours," said Ntare. "Long ago, strange men from the north – I call them men although some thought they were evil gods – with white skins and great wickedness in their hearts forced the people to the south to dig in the ground and bring up this gold. For many years they did this and took the gold north with them. The southern people cared nothing for the gold. But the strange northern men beat the people and raped their women. And they took many slaves back to the north."

Micombero and the other children were spellbound, listening wide-eyed to their father.

"Were these strange men Arabi?" asked Micombero.

"More wicked even than the Arabi," answered Ntare. "They were called Ma-Iti."

"How comes the gold to be here, Father?" asked Micombero. "I found it in a hole in the rocks by the stream."

"The people to the south rose up in rebellion one day," explained Ntare. "They killed many of the evil Ma-Iti. Some escaped though, and carried the gold into our country. Your grandfather, eleven generations ago, fought them. He and the other warriors killed the Ma-Iti. But the Ma-Iti must have hidden this gold before they died."

"What makes the gold nasty? That the Ma-Iti were so cruel in taking it?"

"Yes, and that's why we must hide it again. If the Arabi come to know of it, they will risk even the wrath of our warriors to get it."

Ntare picked up the nugget with a scrap of tanned skin and put it safely out of reach of the children. Then he went in search of the other boys' fathers. After conferring with them, they sought out the shaman and arranged for a cleansing ceremony for their sons. Then they had the boys show them where the cache of gold was and retrieved it, being careful not to touch it.

One early morning Ntare, Micombero, the other boys and their fathers followed the shaman to the site of the cleansing ceremony. As they dug a deep hole, the shaman donned his long, colorful mask and began to chant an incantation over the gold piled nearby. Once the hole was dug, they all hunkered around it. The shaman continued to chant and wave various charms over the gold. The spell of protection cast, he signaled to the men and boys to throw the gold into the hole and cover it up. They tramped the dirt down well and the shaman said another incantation over the spot. He led the way back, the boys and their fathers walking in pairs.

"See, Micombero," said Ntare cheerfully, "no harm will come now because of the gold."

"The shaman's charms have removed the curse from us?"

"Yes. Now we are all purified from the touch of the stuff and we can go home without bringing trouble to the women and piccanins."

"I was afraid I had brought great evil on them, Father," said Micombero soberly.

"I know. And so it might have been if you hadn't showed me the gold so we could get the shaman's help in time. I'm very proud of you, my son."

Micombero's heart swelled with love and

gladness as Ntare put his arm around his shoulders.

Shortly after the purification ceremony, it was decided to go on a trading expedition. Micombero was bitterly disappointed not to be allowed to accompany the men but Ntare told him that he was yet too young; he could go when he was twelve. With that Micombero had to be content.

Ntare made preparations for the trip, which would be a lengthy one. He sat in the dooryard one day, carefully checking his spear and affixing a new spearhead. He sighted down the shaft, turning it slowly to make sure it was still straight and true. The children were playing around him while his three wives wove mats and baskets, one with an infant in her lap, another pregnant.

Ntare finished with his spear and looked around, smiling at his family. The children noticed that his attention was on them and gathered around him. The two smallest ones climbed into his lap. He held out his arms and his wife brought the infant to him.

"Today," he said, "I'm going to tell you the story of how a handsome young husband took his lovely new wife to the love mat and…"

Mbonimana interrupted hastily. "Ntare," she said sternly, "not that story for the piccanins."

"Not?" Ntare feigned great amazement. He

looked around at his family, all of whom were laughing. He laughed with them. "One day," he began again, "a lovely young woman, perfect of face and form, was walking through the forest. It was just after the time of the rains and the forest was glistening green and smelled newly-bathed. This was Marimba, Mother of Music. As she walked, listening to the calls of the birds and watching the dew sparkle and shimmer in the sun, she spied a group of boys. They were looking at something on the ground.

"Marimba wondered what they had been up to for they were very quiet and everyone knows that boys are only quiet when they've been up to mischief. Marimba was very angry when she saw what these boys had done. A little antelope doe, heavy with young, had been strangled in the noose of a trap.

"Marimba demanded to know which of the boys had done that cruel and evil thing. At last one of the boys spoke up and admitted his guilt. That night, under the rising moon, Marimba took her place on the Rock of Justice. The trial ended in the boy's conviction of inventing a new thing, which is reserved only to the gods, and of wantonly taking life. He was thrown to the crocodiles."

The children were wide-eyed and somber as

they contemplated the meaning of the story. The idea of being thrown to the crocodiles was horrifying. Mbonimana waited a couple of minutes to let them absorb the moral then went into the hut and returned with a marimba. She placed it on the ground in front of Ntare and waited expectantly. The children grinned delightedly and watched their father hopefully.

"And," Ntare added, "Marimba used the trap to fashion a new musical instrument."

He handed the baby to Mbonimana, took up the mallets and began to play. The children hopped up and began to dance.

That evening Ntare and Mbonimana walked along the stream.

"There are no more skins to make loincloths or skirts," Mbonimana said.

"And, as usual, everyone needs new clothes?"

"Yes, of course. Maybe you can trade the ivory for lion skins."

"If it were not forbidden, I would dress you in cheetah skin." Ntare noticed that Mbonimana seemed quiet and preoccupied. "Are you worried about the trip?"

"No, not exactly worried. Sometimes I wonder what would become of us all if you were killed."

"There is no need to wonder," Ntare laughed. "I will not be killed. My destiny is to live to be a very old toothless and wrinkled elder, one of great wisdom. I shall beget more than a hundred piccanins and they will brighten our old age, yours and mine."

"I am also to live to such a great age?"

Ntare stopped and looked deeply into her eyes. He put his arms around her, holding her to his heart.

"Mbonimana, without you to give me strength and joy, how could I even care to live?"

"The others have not taken my place in your heart?"

Ntare was surprised. "I thought you knew that you are the dearest of my wives. The bride of my youth, the mother of my firstborn son."

"I should have known that you would not forget. Only, sometimes, you are so busy with the others…"

"Never think that. Never suppose me capable of forgetting what you mean to me."

He kissed her repeatedly, passionately, all over her face, except for her lips. She smiled happily and threw her arms around him with such exuberance that they both fell into the stream. They sat up in shock at the cold water, looked at each other, laughed and splashed and began to play like children.

It was early in the morning when Ntare was ready to start on the trading trip. The first pale streaks of false dawn showed in the east. His whole family surrounded him, Micombero holding his spear. The elephant tusk that he would use for barter was wrapped in special matting, waiting by the gate.

"Are you never going to wean the child?" he teasingly asked the wife who held her infant in her arms. Until the child was weaned there could be no physical intimacy between husband and wife.

The wife was embarrassed but pleased. "It's much too soon."

He grinned at her, kissed her cheek and went to his pregnant wife. He embraced her tenderly.

"Today is a good day for bringing my son into the world," Ntare told her.

"Perhaps he'll be here when you return," she smiled.

Instantly, Ntare was serious. "Have you had pains?"

The wife laughed. "Not yet. Anyone would think this was to be your firstborn."

Ntare laughed, too. "Not if he looked around him."

He smiled and kissed her cheek. Mbonimana had been watching tolerantly; he took her in his arms.

"Remember, if you go swimming," he began.

Mbonimana interrupted, laughing. "Yes, I know. Watch out for crocodiles."

Ntare laughed and kissed her on both cheeks. He hugged her again. Then he took his spear from Micombero and, smiling around at all his family, picked up the tusk and began the long march to the trading site.

As he walked, Ntare met others from the village who were also going on the trading trip, laden with their goods. They camped out on the savanna that night, happy with their progress that day, looking forward to bringing back the skins and other goods that were needed. They were asleep when the faint sound of a warning drum came across the savanna. It was quickly silenced. Ntare woke and sat up, alarmed. He looked around but saw nothing unusual until he raised his head to look farther afield. The hills were dotted with fires that he knew to be burning houses.

"No," he screamed, jumping to his feet. "No, no, no. It can't be. No, no, no."

The other warriors leaped to their feet and followed his gaze to the hills. Leaving their trade goods, taking nothing but their weapons, they began to run toward home.

Knowing what he would find in no way lessened the shock when Ntare finally stood in his dooryard again. The house was still smoldering and the dead bodies of his family lay all around him. The little children had been killed and tossed aside but Micombero and the women had been tortured before they were killed. Ntare fell to his knees, his hands clasped behind his head, and screamed his rage and grief, his body twisting with agony. His scream was echoed from other dooryards all across the hillside.

Revenge was an important component of the tribe's philosophy. When Ntare and the other warriors had performed the last services they could for their dead, they gathered to discuss what they would do next. They knew that their families had been killed by Arab raiders so the only real question was where to strike at the Arabs. They took up their weapons and moved north, grim and silent.

At an oasis, unsuspecting of the danger that stalked them, a small group of Arabs camped. The party was escorting a princess to the court of a neighboring sheik, as his bride. The camels and horses were picketed and sentinels were posted.

Inside the largest, most luxurious tent, the bride reclined on a cushioned couch. This was Starla, once more a leading figure in Pat Mayhew's past life. There were rugs on the floor, chests of fine clothes, all the accoutrements of a

84

rich and royal progress. The bride wore a long, flowing skirt and a fitted bodice with a great many golden ornaments. Neither she nor any of her women wore face veils, that fashion not having arrived as yet.

As one of the women served the princess a dish of figs and a cup of wine, the noise of battle erupted outside. There was a long, drawn-out scream then much running and shouting. The women began to run about, hampering each other in their efforts to conceal the princess and her casket of jewels. One of the women had the presence of mind to cut a slit in the back of the tent and the princess slipped through it.

There was pandemonium outside. Hand-to-hand fighting was fierce and several of the black warriors fell. But in the end all the Arab men were killed. As was their custom, the warriors plundered the camp of everything they could use. They cut the horses and camels loose and dragged the women from their hiding places.

Ntare was running with a torch, setting fire to the tents when he caught a slight movement behind the largest tent. The princess was cautiously moving from the rear of the tent toward the palm trees that fringed the springs. The light of the torch fell on her and she turned, her eyes wide with terror. She saw Ntare and ran. He threw the torch into the tent and gave chase. He caught her in the shadow of the palms and threw her to the ground.

She fought him wildly but his strength was too much for her. He took his knife from the scabbard at his side and slit the fastening of her bodice. He plunged the knife into the sand just out of her reach. But the terror in the princess' eyes triggered Ntare's memory of his dead wives. As she recited prayers, Ntare found that, after all, he could not violate a woman, even an Arab.

He rolled over to lie face down in the sand, his head cradled in his arms. The princess was incredulous but hesitated only a split second before seizing the knife. As she did so, Ntare turned over, saw what she was doing and thumped his chest, over his heart.

"Yes," he hissed. "Do it. Strike here."

The princess raised the knife and was about to stab Ntare when two warriors, Mutaga and Misage, bounded toward them. Ntare leaped to his feet and grabbed the knife from the girl. Misage lunged at the princess but Ntare stepped between them, seizing her by the wrist, holding the knife so it threatened Misage.

"What are you doing, Ntare?" Misage was astonished. "She was going to kill you."

"I wish she had," Ntare replied bitterly.

Mutaga glowered at the Arab girl. "We'll teach her what happens to Arabi who meddle with our people."

"No." Ntare made a small but effective gesture at Mutaga with the knife. "She is my captive."

"She was going to kill you," Mutaga said, incredulous that Ntare was protecting an Arab. "What's wrong with you? Have you gone crazy?"

Misage, too, could not believe Ntare's attitude. "Have you forgotten what the Arabi did to our women? If you have, I have not. I remember what they did to my wives and daughters. Now the same shall happen to theirs."

"Not to this one," Ntare said.

"To all of them," said Misage fiercely. "I would wipe the Arabi from the face of the earth."

"You know the law, Ntare," said Mutaga. "We will avenge our dead."

'Vengeance I shall have," agreed Ntare. "But not on this woman."

Misage concluded that Ntare was indeed crazy and moved to take the girl from him. In a flash, Ntare let go of her and struck, sinking the knife to the hilt in Misage's stomach. He withdrew the blade as Misage sagged to his knees. Mutaga backed away, convinced that Ntare was possessed of a devil. He turned and ran back to the blazing camp. The girl stooped to pull Misage's knife clear of its sheath. Before she could strike him, Ntare used the haft of his own knife to knock it out of her hand. He caught her by the wrist again.

"Don't be stupid," he said to her contemptuously. "How could you live without me now? You'd starve in the first week. If some of my brothers-in-arms didn't find you first."

He sheathed his knife and led her away, keeping to the shadows of the palms as long as he could. She held the cut edges of her bodice together with her free hand. When they were some distance out in the desert, Ntare stopped and looked back at the Arab camp. It was still burning but the warriors were leaving, going in single file, carrying their dead and wounded.

The next morning, at dawn, Ntare led the princess back to the ravaged camp. It was bleak and ugly in the rosy first light. The tents were still smoldering and the Arab dead lay where they had fallen. The princess averted her eyes from the corpses as Ntare dragged her along with him. All at once, she jerked free and ran toward a scimitar that was laying in the sand. Ntare grabbed her. She glared at him, then, realizing that her bodice was open, pulled the edges together and held them.

"The Arabi are even stupider than I've been told. I wonder how you expect to live if you run away or kill me. Or maybe you think to kill yourself?"

The girl struggled to free herself, pulling and twisting against his grip.

"Enough. Cease." Ntare was losing patience.

He found a length of light rope and passed it around her waist, tying it securely behind her. He made a loop at the other end and slipped it over his hand. She backed away from him as far as the rope would allow.

Ntare grinned suddenly. "Cease. That's a good name for you. Niboyu. I wonder if you are too stupid to learn to answer to it." He yanked on the rope. "Niboyu."

The girl ignored him. He yanked again.

"Niboyu."

She looked at him contemptuously.

"Good," he said. "That's some progress. Niboyu." He tugged at the rope. 'Come, Niboyu."

Sullenly, she advanced a couple of paces toward him.

"That's fine, Niboyu."

Ntare began to search the camp for anything that would be useful in what he knew was going to be a long hard-fought battle for survival. Niboyu followed him without being pulled. He picked up a couple of water gourds and handed them to her. She let them fall, making no effort to hold them. He jerked the rope and pointed at the gourds, glaring at her.

"The woman's an idiot. Niboyu, pick up the water bottles. Do you want to die of thirst in this forsaken sheet of sand? Take good care of the water bottles or that is what will happen to you."

Slowly, unwillingly, Niboyu picked up the water gourds. They had thongs attached so they could be slung over the shoulder, but she merely held them by the thongs.

Ntare found his spear near the back of the big tent's ruins and picked it up, testing it to see that the shaft was sound and the spearhead unbroken. Niboyu gingerly picked through the rubble and found her jewel casket. Ntare turned to see her pick it up.

"Niboyu."

Reluctantly, suspiciously, Niboyu approached him.

"What is that?" he demanded.

He took the casket from her and opened it. Seeing that it was filled with golden jewelry, he made a sound of disgust and threw it as far out into the pool as he could. Niboyu grabbed at his arm and tried to stop him but he shook her off. He looked down at her where she'd fallen and it finally registered that she was wearing many jewels. He pulled her to her feet, unfastened the golden necklace she was wearing and threw it into the pool. One by one, he stripped her bracelets and rings from her and threw them away. That puzzled her greatly.

He took the water gourds and filled them, handing them back to her to carry. She considered defying him but decided not to. He started off at a lope and she followed, trying to keep some slack in the rope.

Later that day, as the sun reached its zenith, Ntare called a halt under an ancient, twisted olive tree at the base of an escarpment. Niboyu was very tired and she plopped down, taking the water gourds off her shoulders and placing them beside her. She carefully held her bodice together. Ntare squatted and surveyed the surrounding countryside. He opened one of the water gourds and drank, then offered it to Niboyu. She drank and put the stopper back in the gourd.

"If we are not to starve, Niboyu, I must go hunting. But what to do with you? You are so stupid you will probably run away if I leave you here. Yet I can't guard you and hunt at the same time."

He took the rope from his wrist and tied her hands securely behind her. Then he climbed the tree and fastened the rope to a branch. He jumped to the ground and, taking his spear, disappeared around a shoulder of the escarpment. Niboyu struggled to free herself but could not even loosen her rope. Her wrists were raw and bleeding when she finally gave up. She had come far in accepting Ntare's dominance by the time he returned late in the afternoon, carrying the hindquarters of an addax antelope fawn.

Niboyu heard his approach and jumped to her feet, instantly alert and alarmed. Ntare laid the meat on a large rock and examined her bonds. He untied her and gently washed the blood away. Taking a piece of fat from the meat, he used it to salve her wrists. Then he began to gather sticks.

"This is women's work, Niboyu," he said. "We need a fire to cook this meat. And also because it will soon be dark and cold. See, Niboyu, pick up the sticks and put them in a pile."

He put a couple of twigs in her hand, moved it over the pile he'd started, and opened her fingers so that the twigs dropped.

"See, it's perfectly easy. You do it."

Sullenly, she did as he bid her, finding sticks and twigs. While she was doing that, Ntare took a flint from his pouch and struck it over the handful of dry grass he'd placed near the wood. He blew on the grass until it flamed, then fed twigs into it until the fire was sufficiently well started to lay the cookfire.

He cut several slices of meat from the venison, then sharpened several sticks and stuck them in the ground near the fire. He hung the meat from the sticks and sat down to wait. The meat juices dripped into the fire, making a delicious aroma. After what seemed hours to both of them, the meat was ready. Hardly waiting for it to cool enough not to burn their mouths, they each took a slice and began to eat. When the first pangs of hunger had been stayed, Ntare began to think aloud.

"Now what to do? I think we will not be pursued. My people think I am a madman – and maybe I am. I don't know why I killed my friend instead of letting him take you. The Arabi will pursue the warriors when they find the camp at the oasis – if so be the Arabi are not too cowardly to seek vengeance."

When their hunger had been satisfied, Ntare set more meat to cook in order to save as much as possible from spoiling in the heat of the next day. He scowled at the desert around him.

"I'm not going to live in this wilderness. But if I return to the hills, my people will kill you. And me, as well, probably."

He watched Niboyu in silence for a few minutes. She untwisted a length of rope and looked around for a sharp rock. Finding one, she sawed the rope across it until it was cut through. She used the strand of rope to fasten her bodice, lacing it down the center. Satisfied, she sat looking into the fire, seemingly oblivious of him.

"I wonder if you could be taught to speak a civilized tongue. Niboyu, pay attention." He waved the strip of meat in his hand at her. "Meat. Say it, Niboyu. Meat."

She looked up and stared at him stonily. He picked up his knife and waved it. Wariness flickered in her eyes.

"Knife. Knife."

Niboyu watched him but did not speak.

He put more wood on the fire. "Fire," he said, pointing to the flames. "Fire."

Ntare looked at her in exasperation. She stared back expressionlessly.

"Tree," he said, pointing. "Niboyu. Say it. Tree."

Niboyu showed no reaction.

"I don't know whether you're too stupid or too stubborn to speak," Ntare exclaimed. "Niboyu. My patience is not inexhaustible." He pointed to the fire. "Fire. Fire!"

Disinterestedly, without moving from her seat, she picked up a few sticks and threw them on the fire. Ntare shook his head and gave it up. He started to go to her but she, seeing him moving toward her, leaped to her feet, prepared to run. He grasped her arm, looking at her with a mixture of sadness and annoyance. He laid down near the fire, pulling her down beside him, between himself and the fire. She resisted but he held her firmly.

"Niboyu," he scolded, "quit your foolishness. I don't choose to let the desert night chill me, whatever you prefer. Lie still and go to sleep."

He prodded her until she lay with her back to him. He curved his body around her and fell asleep almost at once. Niboyu lay rigidly awake far into the night.

For days Ntare and Niboyu traveled in a southerly direction through the desert toward a more hospitable country. As they went they were learning to accommodate to one another's needs and puzzling over the differences in the ways they went about camp life. Late one afternoon they camped under an escarpment and sat in the shade of the overhanging rock. Niboyu's hair was disheveled and her skirt was torn and hanging almost in shreds. She watched curiously as Ntare carved a piece of wood. Whatever he was making was about four inches wide and six inches long, with most of the length in tines. He was nearly finished carving patterns into the solid part. As he worked, he talked.

95

"You need new clothes. Those are very bedraggled and totally unsuited to living like this. A good lion skin skirt would be much more practical and attractive. Why do Arabi women cover their breasts? It's an ugly custom as well as being morally repugnant."

He put his knife back in its sheath and rubbed his fingers across the carving. Smiling in satisfaction, he tossed it to her. She caught it and turned it over and over, examining the carvings of animals. She looked at him questioningly. He went to her and took it.

"It's for your hair," he explained. "A comb will make it easy to keep the tangles out."

He ran the comb through her hair, gently teasing the tangles until they loosened and her hair fell about her shoulders in long tresses. She motioned for him to sit beside her. He sat and she took the comb from him. She stood behind him and touched his tight black curls wonderingly. Tentatively, she pushed the comb into his hair; to her surprise the comb ran through it easily. She sat back down beside him, fingering the comb.

"There's a small Arabi encampment nearby," he said softly. "I think it's due for a taste of my vengeance. I will return when I have dealt with them."

Ntare rose and, taking his spear, left the camp.

96

Keeping to the shade of the escarpment as long as he could, he loped toward the Arabi camp.

The small group of Arabi had pitched their two tents near a tiny water hole. In the long shadows of evening, the sheep and goats were grazing on the sparse grass nearby, watched by the herd boys. Ntare lay on his stomach on a hillock a little distance away, watching the activity in the camp.

There was a man squatting in front of one of the tents brewing coffee. A group of chattering women and girls was sitting in front of the other tent, sewing and spinning. Children and dogs played all around. Only one horse was visible, a mare tied to a tent rope, wearing an ornate saddle and bridle. As Ntare watched, a second man joined the coffee-brewer who poured the dark liquid into tiny handleless cups, handing one to the newcomer. Ntare crept forward, carefully preserving the advantage of his surprise. The dogs discovered him first and began to bark hysterically, followed almost immediately by the children who began to yell and scream.

Instantly, everyone looked around, trying to see where the threat was lurking. Ntare hurled his spear at one of the men, catching him in the stomach as he was in the act of rising. The other man ran to cut loose the mare, slapping her on the rump to send her out of danger. The women

97

shrieked and ran to the children, gathering them up to run out into the desert to hide. Two young girls, terrified, peered out of one of the tents, too frightened to leave the tent but knowing that it was no protection. A small boy stood in front of the tent, watching Ntare, his eyes wide with fear but with a hard glint of courage in the depths.

Having sent the mare out of harm's way, the Arabi man grasped his scimitar and prepared to do battle. Ntare pulled his spear out of the first man but it was stuck in a bone. The momentary delay allowed the Arab to slash at him but Ntare was able to parry the blow with the shaft of his spear. The scimitar cut the shaft in two near the spearhead, leaving Ntare with only his knife to fight with.

Taking each other's measure, Ntare and the Arab circled slowly. The Arab made a sudden lurch, slicing within a millimeter of Ntare's ribs. Before he could recover his guard, Ntare struck upwards and the blade of his knife sliced into his enemy's jugular vein. Skipping aside to avoid the gush of blood, Ntare watched as the man dropped his scimitar and fell beside it. He turned away and picked up his spearhead. He cut it loose from the stump of the spear and dropped it into his pouch. Then he entered the tent.

The two girls were cowering together at the

rear of the tent, crouched behind a chest that was completely inadequate to hide them. Ntare glanced at them once then ignored them as they ran, panic-stricken, out of the tent. He opened the chest and began to rummage through the clothing inside. He held up a skirt, rejected it and found another. The second one was of lightweight wool, embroidered with silver thread. He tossed aside the bodices he found but decided to take a light-weight woolen head veil and a thick woolen blanket.

Ntare was making a bundle of his booty when the small boy entered the tent. He was carrying the scimitar but it was all he could do to lift it. Ntare grinned at the little warrior as he advanced grimly with the scimitar. As he tried to swing the weapon, Ntare caught him up in his arms, taking it away and throwing it aside. With a length of cord, he bound the boy's hands and feet, gently but securely. The boy fought as best he could and bit Ntare a couple of times. Admiring the child's courage, he refrained from retaliation. He finished tying up his bundle and went outside.

The moon was high when he approached his own camp. He circled around to the top of the escarpment. As he looked over, he could see Niboyu below, sitting serenely, waiting patiently. Beside her was a big pile of sticks for the fire.

Ntare untied his bundle and dropped the skirt and head veil into Niboyu's lap. Startled, she jumped to her feet, looking for whoever was above her on the rock.

Ntare laughed and leaped down to her. He tossed the blanket aside and took the skirt from her, shaking it out so she could see the pretty, shiny embroidery. Niboyu became very excited and apprehensive, using sign and body language to ask if he'd killed the woman who wore the skirt. Finally, he understood. He made such signs as he could to tell her that he had not.

"No," he said, "I didn't kill the owner. It's all right."

His smile reassured her. She pointed to her ragged bodice and looked a question at him. He shook his head. He held the skirt out to her and she took it but made no move to exchange her rags for it. He mimed putting on the skirt, wrapping the veil around his head. She just looked at him.

He sighed. "I suppose I'll have to strip the old clothes off and put the new ones on her myself. I never saw such a stupid woman."

He took the skirt from her and held it to her waist. She snatched it from him and stamped her foot, pointing at him.

Her meaning dawned on him. "Oh. Maybe I'm

the stupid one this time."

Ntare turned and left the camp, walking along the foot of the escarpment, thinking of Mbonimana and his dead family. Grief racked his being, a grief so deep that he knew he would never be free of it. Nor did he want to be. The thought of the possibility of a cessation of his grief brought a stab of pain. To cease grieving would, he felt confusedly, be like turning his back on his wives and children. It would be like deserting them in their most terrible need.

When he returned to camp, Niboyu had donned the new skirt and wrapped the head veil around her head and shoulders. But she still wore the old raggedy bodice. Ntare flicked it contemptuously. Niboyu turned away from him. He caught her arm and whirled her back to face him, drawing his knife as he did so. Her eyes widened in surprise and a tinge of fear. He slit the rope that held the bodice together and pulled the garment off her body. He tossed it onto the fire and smiled in wry satisfaction. Niboyu looked him in the eyes and removed her head veil, retying it around herself to cover her breasts. Ntare stalked away in disgust.

The next morning, as Ntare led the way through a gully, Niboyu hurried up to him and put her hand on his arm to stop him. She signaled for silence and pointed. Some way ahead of them stood the mare from the Arabi camp, still wearing the saddle and bridle. The mare was watching them uneasily, tossing her head and pecking with one forefoot. Niboyu signaled Ntare to stay where he was. She removed the stopper from one of the water gourds and moved forward, keeping her eyes on the horse.

Very slowly Niboyu approached the mare, speaking softly. The horse danced before her, back and sideways, tossing her head, ready to bolt at the tiniest suspicious movement of the strange human. Niboyu stopped walking but continued to talk softly. The mare quieted and sniffed, smelling the water in the open gourd. Niboyu, with almost imperceptible actions, so slowly did she move, poured a little water into her cupped hand. The mare came forward haltingly, with much anxious side-stepping, desperate for the water that people had always before provided for her. A handful at a time, Niboyu gave the horse all the water in both gourds. By the time the last few drops had been taken, she and the mare were fast friends.

Carefully, so as not to alarm the horse, Niboyu picked up the reins. She stroked the horse's neck, still speaking softly. The mare whinnied and nuzzled the girl's shoulder. Niboyu eased back to the saddle and smiled as the horse looked around but made no objection as she mounted. The animal was still a bit skittish but Niboyu steadied her and rode in a large circle with Ntare in the center. As Niboyu and the mare became comfortable with one another, she urged the horse to more speed, first a trot, then a canter, and finally an all-out gallop. But in only a minute or two, she brought the mare to a dramatic stop in front of Ntare. She knew that the tiny quantity of water that the horse had been able to drink from her hand was not nearly enough for the big animal. They must get her to an oasis quickly.

Ntare also realized that they must find water immediately, not only for the horse but for themselves. Midday was nearly upon them and traveling in the heat of the day would increase their risks. He vaulted onto the horse, in back of the saddle, and pointed the direction for Niboyu to guide the horse.

Some days later, Ntare had mastered the simple art of staying aboard the mare while Niboyu clung to him, riding pillion. He wanted very badly to ride as the Arabi did, showily and daringly, but there wasn't time to practice even if it had been possible to ask the mare to work that hard on short rations and little rest. He knew instinctively that they must care for the mare as best their circumstances would allow – life would be much harder without her.

As swiftly as possible Ntare had pushed across the desert and into the jungle. It was terrain that he knew imperfectly and the woman knew not at all but it was safer than the desert or the highlands. Ntare had cut Niboyu's skirt short in the style of his tribeswomen. It was practical and gave him some small sense of familiarity, even though Niboyu refused to part with the head veil which she continued to wear as a bodice.

As they rode through the jungle, using a footpath that was barely wide enough to accommodate the horse, a jungle fowl hung from the saddle. Ntare had picked it off with a well-thrown rock as it scratched and pecked on a rotting log. He stopped the mare in a small clearing where a rollicking stream cut through the vegetation. Niboyu had seemingly accepted the situation. She slipped to the ground and began to gather wood for a fire. Ntare unsaddled the mare and led her to drink in the stream, tethering her in a spot where she could reach the water and also graze on the rich grass. He turned his attention to Niboyu and was surprised to see that she had a fire laid and was industriously plucking the fowl. He grinned at her, nodding his approval, then drew out his firestarter to make a spark.

That night, after a satisfying meal of roast fowl

and some sort of fruit, the name of which neither of them knew but trusted not to be harmful upon seeing the monkeys eating it, they sat around the campfire for a little while. Presently, Niboyu laid down and closed her eyes. Ntare watched her, thinking sadly of his wives and children. He checked that the mare was secure and threw some wood on the fire. He curled up on the opposite side of the fire from the woman and composed himself for sleep. After a long time, he slept, but lightly; he flung his arms and legs about restlessly.

Niboyu woke and lay watching him over the embers of the fire. She was puzzled at first. His face contorted with the horror of his nightmare. Niboyu sat up, the stirrings of compassion overcoming the tag end of her fear. Ntare began to mutter in his sleep. Only one word was recognizable.

"Mbonimana," he mumbled. He sat up, suddenly wide awake. Tears coursed down his cheeks. He screamed his dead wife's name, "Mbonimana." Seeing Niboyu watching him, he turned away from her. Clasping his hands behind his head he rocked his body to the rhythm of his grief.

Niboyu edged closer to him, overwhelmed by the intensity of his pain. She touched his shoulder and he turned to her. Tears coursed down his cheeks. Niboyu touched his wet cheek gently.

Ntare unclasped his hands and stilled his body. He gazed at her and spoke softly, vehemently. "Yes, even the Arabi woman is moved to compassion by such suffering. Be glad, Niboyu, that you didn't see my wives and piccanins after your cowardly curs finished their butchery. Someday I will tell you their names. Someday you shall hear how they died."

Niboyu put her hand on his arm and he put his arms around her, grateful for her touch, grateful for the small comfort of her presence. He lay back and she nudged him to turn so that his back was to her. Niboyu curved her body around his and in their distresses and tentative reaching out was the beginning of true caring.

Late the next afternoon as they rode through the forest, Ntare glimpsed the movement of a dikdik in the undergrowth. He threw one leg over the mare's neck and slid to the ground. He disappeared into the underbrush, stalking the little deer, and Niboyu scooched over the cantle and into the saddle to ride to a suitable camping spot. It wasn't long until she found a clearing with a stream running through it. She drank deeply then tethered the mare with a long rope that would allow her to graze and to reach the water.

Gathering firewood was her next chore. When she judged she had enough to cook the evening meal and to keep a smudge fire burning through the night, she sat down to wait.

Presently, Ntare came, carrying the dikdik's carcass tied to a short pole slung over his shoulder. Niboyu pointed to the heap of firewood.

"Fire," she said.

Ntare was so startled to hear her speak that he nearly dropped the dikdik. Excitedly, he put the carcass down and leaned his spear against a handy tree. Niboyu jumped to her feet and Ntare caught her up in a happy embrace. She was puzzled by his excitement but glad to see him smile.

"Fire," Ntare repeated. "Yes, fire. We need a fire to cook the venison. Say it again." Ntare grinned at her and shook her gently but insistently.

"Fire?" Niboyu asked doubtfully.

"Fire, fire, fire." Ntare hugged her joyfully. "What else can you say?"

Niboyu put her head on one side and looked him in the eyes. Then she pointed to various objects as she named them. "Meat. Knife. Ntare. Like-a-zebra-but-unlike-a-zebra. Spear. Hand. Stupid."

As she said the last word, she touched her own chest. Ntare laughed and she laughed with him.

"No," he said, with his hand on his own chest, "here is Stupid."

The days wore on, varying little in the struggle to survive. The jungle was not home to either Ntare or Niboyu so it was not easy for them to know which plants were edible. They found fruits of various kinds and watched the monkeys to see which were all right to eat. But edible was not necessarily palatable and they found that the monkeys ate many kinds of fruit that were too bitter for human consumption. But there was lots of game, both bird and mammal.

After some months together, Niboyu spoke Ntare's language quite fluently and what began as enmity had become friendship and, inevitably, had grown into love. When the rainy season set in, they found a cave and settled in for the duration. It was situated above the forest floor, so high that they could see over the canopy to the mountains, far away. One evening they sat near the entrance of the cave, listening to the diurnal birds as they rustled in the trees, preparing to sleep, and the nocturnal birds as they prepared for the night's hunting.

Niboyu touched Ntare's lips with her fingers and looked at him questioningly. "Why is it forbidden to kiss you here?"

Ntare spoke seriously. "Such a kiss is holy."

He looked at her quizzically. "Do you understand 'holy'?"

"Holy?" Niboyu repeated the word, watching his face for clues as to its meaning.

"Sacred. It would offend God, if done profanely."

"There is a time such a kiss may be given?" she asked.

"Only if a piccanin is desired."

Niboyu stood, looking out into the forest for a long moment. She was beautiful in her short lion skin skirt and cloth bodice. She turned and looked deeply into Ntare's eyes, then began to dance. It was a dance of sensuous delight, designed to charm a man. Ntare caught his breath sharply, his love shining in his eyes. Niboyu knelt behind him and put her arms around his shoulders, kissing the back of his neck. He leaned back and she kissed his neck, his ears, his jaw. She moved around to lie in his arms and Ntare kissed her eyes. But when she nearly touched his lips with hers, he turned his face aside. Niboyu sat up.

"Is it because I am Arabi?" she whispered in her hurt.

"I have forgotten that you are not of my people."

'Why, then?"

"You're a slave."

Niboyu was shocked. "A slave? Me? Never. I would die rather than be enslaved."

She sprang to her feet. Ntare stood and looked at her sadly.

"Niboyu. I took you in battle and carried you away in bonds. I have made a slave of you. And I know now that I never want to father a piccanin on a slave woman. My children must be free."

Niboyu looked around wildly and saw the knife where he had left it, beside a piece of tanned antelope skin. She seized it and he reached her to knock it from her hands just before she plunged it into her heart. He tried to comfort her but she broke away and dashed out of the cave, down the path and into the jungle. He followed, alternately commanding and pleading with her to stop.

Niboyu ran, not caring where she went, desperate to escape the dreadful thing that Ntare had said. The words beat into her brain: "You're a slave, you're a slave, you're a slave."

All at once the ground fell away and she plummeted into a leopard trap. She lay at the bottom, the breath knocked out of her. As she gasped and fought for air, Ntare peered over the edge. He waited until she was breathing normally again before he spoke.

"Niboyu," he said, "listen to me."

She ignored him.

"Niboyu! Stop being an idiot and stand up."

Niboyu stood up, tears streaming down her face, refusing to look at him. "Yes, Master."

That made Ntare angry. "That's enough of that. I should leave you here. You've spoiled these people's leopard trap and no doubt they'll be angry enough to punish you as you deserve."

"Leopard trap?" she quavered, trying to pretend indifference. Her tears ceased and she wiped her eyes.

"Perhaps I should leave you for bait and let the leopard find you. I would but I love you."

She looked at him then. "A warrior in love with an Arabi slave girl? Have you no pride?"

"Not as much as you."

"A slave with pride? You must beat me into a proper submissiveness, then."

"You tempt me."

"Go ahead," she flared. "There's nothing to stop you. Not in my law or yours."

Ntare forebore to answer but went to cut a stout vine. He tied one end around a nearby tree and dropped the other end down to Niboyu.

"Come out of there," he ordered.

Niboyu climbed up the vine and Ntare stooped to pull her over the edge of the pit. He kissed her face and her hands, which were bleeding from the vine. She accepted his caresses meekly enough

111

but he could not gauge her feelings. Uneasily but tenderly, he escorted her back to the cave.

Ntare cut some strips from the soft, tanned antelope skin and used them to bandage Niboyu's hands. He sat down and pulled her onto his lap. Exhausted by her emotional outburst, she laid her head on his shoulder.

"Is it your belief that there will be no piccanins if we do not kiss each other's lips?" she asked.

"What an ignorant little barbarian you are," he smiled. "No, it is not the kissing that causes the piccanins."

"What are we to do? Will you send me away?"

"Never." Ntare tightened his arms around her. "I must present the brideprice to your father. If he lives. Was he killed in the fight at the oasis?"

"He wasn't there. He had arranged for me to marry a neighboring sheik. Those were mostly the sheik's men you killed."

"Then we must go to your father. Only, I don't see what I'm to use as bridewealth."

"There's the mare."

"Yes," Ntare said sarcastically, "that would be a fine thing – to use the woman's own wealth for her brideprice."

Niboyu considered for a moment. "You could steal horses from another caravan."

Ntare laughed. "That would be funny. To steal

112

the bridewealth from the Arabi."

He set her off his lap and laid down, pulling her down to lie cuddled against him.

"Go to sleep now; we must start at first light."

"I love you," she said softly.

A few minutes later she spoke again, more softly still. "I wonder where the leopard is."

Ntare smiled and his arm tightened around her.

At first light they saddled the mare and set out for the desert. They rode for many days, first through the jungle and then through the desert. Finally, they came upon a small Arabi camp at a tiny oasis. Niboyu and the mare stood in the shadow of a cliff in the twilight, watching Ntare. Carrying his spear, he slipped silently across the sand toward the tents.

There were only three tents and each had a mare tied to a front tent rope. In the dim light of a first quarter moon, Ntare glided up to the first tent and untied the mare's lead. The horses were uneasy at his approach, pawing and tossing their heads, but it was not until he reached the third horse that one of them whinnied. As if that were a signal, the dogs began to bark. They converged on Ntare, growling threateningly and baring their teeth at him. Ntare jerked the lead rope on the third mare loose and mounted her bareback.

A man stumbled sleepily out of the center tent,

saw Ntare and shouted to awaken the other men. He seized a scimitar and lunged at Ntare. Ntare dropped the leads of the two horses and grasped his spear in fighting fashion. He spun the mare around and rode at the man with the scimitar. The man dropped the knife and flattened himself on the ground. As the tents disgorged their occupants, men shouting, women screaming, and children wailing, Ntare yelled his battle cry and whirled the mare to race through the encampment again. The two loose horses ran out into the desert, frightened and excited. Ntare galloped after them, grinning at the success of his little raid.

Once well clear of the camp, Ntare slowed the mare to a walk and finally let her stop. He sat on her, watching her ears for signs that she heard her companions. It wasn't long before her right ear began to swivel around and she turned her head to the right and stared eagerly into the dark. She whickered softly and one of the mares came slowly forward, stretching her neck to verify the identity of Ntare's horse. They greeted each other, Ntare keeping still and silent. The two horses relaxed and Ntare allowed them time to become used to his presence. Then he reached down to pick up the lead rope of the loose mare. She took a step backwards but allowed him to capture her.

He nudged his mare forward.

As he headed back toward the foot of the cliff where he'd left Niboyu, he could hear the other loose mare off to one side. He knew that the spring at the bottom of the cliff would bring her and wasted no effort in chasing her.

Niboyu heard the sound of hooves and sprang to her feet. She swung herself up into the saddle and rode out to meet Ntare. When she saw that he was riding one horse and leading another, she urged her mount into a mad gallop and rode toward him. Ntare pressed his mare forward and galloped directly at Niboyu. At the last possible second they both swerved, laughing delightedly. Ntare dropped his spear and the rope of the mare he was leading and he and Niboyu reverted to childhood and galloped a fantastic fandango on the moonlit sands.

They rode figure eights, they reared their horses, they spun tight little circles – and then it happened. They galloped toward one another, closer and closer. Niboyu's mare fell to one knee, her foot deep in a rodent's hole. It seemed to Ntare that Niboyu and the mare moved in slow motion, the horse falling, Niboyu flying out of the saddle. The mare struggled out of the hole but the woman lay motionless on the sand.

Ntare slid to the ground and ran to her. He fell

to his knees beside her and cradled her head against his chest. He sat nearly as motionless as she until the sun rose. He scooped out a grave in the sand, laid her gently in it and covered her. He knelt there, his face raised to the skies, mutely asking questions to which there were no answers.

With precise deliberation, he pulled his knife out of its sheath and plunged it into his heart.

Part III

The Pirate Captain

Dr. Parker was taking notes as Pat lay in the recliner, deep in a regressive trance, describing his situation.

"The captain says the wind is fair; we should reach Barbados in a few days," Pat said, smiling.

"Why are you going to Barbados?" Dr. Parker asked.

"Actually, I'm going to Carolina. I'm sick of London. First the Black Death, then the fire. My brother is in Carolina and he says everything's fresh and clean and any man may make his fortune."

"You mean the Great London Fire?"

"It was great, right enough. They say His Majesty himself joined in the fighting of it."

"King...Charles?" Dr. Parker tried to gather her historical references together in her mind. "What year is it?"

"1668. Yes, of course King Charles. The Second."

"Did you fight the fire?"

"Aye. And ruined a brand-new greatcoat in doing it. It was a sight, that fire. It seemed all

London was aflame."

"Tell me about yourself," suggested Dr. Parker. "Are you a gentleman?"

"Aye. A gentleman and a scholar. I'm a physician."

"A surgeon?"

"A physician," Pat repeated testily. "What next? 'Pothecary?"

"I'm sorry I'm so ignorant," Dr. Parker apologized. "What's the difference between a physician and a surgeon?"

"Surgeons do the rough work, such as amputations. Physicians diagnose ailments and prescribe medicines."

"Thank you. Are you married, Doctor? I don't know your name."

"No, nor much of anything else, seemingly. My name is Henry Cooper. Dr. Henry Cooper. At your service, madam."

"Are you married, Dr. Cooper?"

"No, nor likely to be," he said, laughing ironically. "And be made a cuckold? No, I've no intention of letting any woman decorate me with a pair of horns."

"Horns? I don't understand."

"God's teeth and eyeballs, woman," Pat exclaimed, exasperated. "Horns! Such as my Lord Castlemaine wears that his wife and the King wrought on him."

He held his fingers up to his forehead to illustrate horns.

Dr. Parker eyed him quizzically. "Let's move ahead to the time you landed at Barbados."

"We never did land at Barbados."

"Why not?"

Dr. Henry Cooper leaned lazily against the rail, watching a sailor in the ship's rigging. Henry was fashionably dressed in knee breeches, a soft shirt with ruffles and lace, a coat that was wonderfully worked with gold braid, and a hat with a mass of plumes. A sword hung at his side.

The ship was a caravel with two masts lateen-rigged and a third mast square-rigged. As the rest of the crew had their duties in sailing the ship, so Leslie, the cabin boy, (who would, in due time, incarnate as Starla Mayhew) had his duties. At the moment he was engaged in carrying a trencher of beef and bread from the galley to the captain's quarters. Watching him was a passenger named Holcombe. Leslie went down the companionway with his trencher and reappeared a few minutes later with an empty jug. Holcombe stepped in front of the companionway, blocking Leslie's passage.

"Please, sir, I must pass," Leslie said, looking

around nervously for support.

Henry heard and looked around, scowling as he saw Holcombe try to kiss the boy.

Leslie dodged the embrace. "No, please, sir, I'm not a lad of that sort."

Holcombe smiled at him. "Come now, Leslie, I can make things very pleasant for you, if you're nice to me."

He caught the boy and kissed him wetly, forcing his mouth open. Leslie struggled but with small effect. He dropped the jug and it rolled across the deck. Henry's disgust boiled over. He pulled Holcombe away, freeing Leslie, who scurried out of reach.

Holcombe rounded on Henry furiously and aimed his fist to strike Henry in the face. Henry ducked and delivered a fierce jab to his stomach. Holcombe staggered back a couple of steps and drew his sword. Henry drew his.

Several sailors crowded around to watch the fight. Henry drew first blood with a trifling wound to the arm. Holcombe succeeded in pinking Henry's hand before Henry pierced his guard and drove his blade between a couple of floating ribs. Holcombe dropped his sword and fell to the deck where he lay conscious and furious. Henry wiped his blade casually on Holcombe's breeches and sheathed it. He wrapped his handkerchief around his wound and strolled away. Leslie gazed after him adoringly, then picked up his jug and clattered down the galley companionway. The sailors grinned and two of them picked Holcombe up and carried him down the after companionway.

That night, as Henry lay in his bunk, watching the stars through his porthole, a soft noise alerted him. He sat up and looked at the door. The moon had not yet risen and, except where the starlight fell on the bed, it was very dark inside the cabin. He could just make out the opening and closing of the door.

"Who is it?" he demanded, his hand on the knife under his pillow.

"Please, sir, it's me, Leslie," came the soft response.

"Leslie?" he repeated, surprised.

"I've come to repay you for what you did for me this afternoon, sir."

"Well, Leslie," Henry said in a low tone, "thank you for your kindness but I'm not a lad of that sort either."

Leslie moved closer to the bunk. He untied his shirt and slipped it over his head. He sat down on the bunk, took Henry's free hand, and placed it on his breast. Henry's astonishment was complete. The knife clattered to the floor.

"You're not a lad at all," he exclaimed.

122

Leslie laughed nearly soundlessly. She untied the ribbon that held her hair clubbed back and shook her head. Her hair, freed of restraint, framed her face. Henry marveled that he'd ever thought her a boy. She slipped her breeches off.

"Oh, Leslie," breathed Henry. He held the covers up so she could slide into bed beside him.

Sometime later, as they lay in the afterglow, Henry's curiosity took a different tack.

"How have you managed to keep your secret as long as this?" he asked.

"Nobody's interested in the cabin boy, sir."

"That's not entirely true. Holcombe was."

"He was the only one."

"Why did you ship on this voyage in the first place?"

Leslie's nose wrinkled with remembered distaste. "I was tired of having to defend myself from men whose ardor outstripped their chivalry. I thought if I masqueraded as a boy, I would be safe."

"You've no father or brother to defend you?"

"My father and mother died in the plague three years ago. I have a brother but he fled to the country and I've not seen him since."

"And in all of London you couldn't find a protector?"

"Indeed, sir, I did. But I found I didn't care for

whoring."

"It's good enough for Nelly Gwynne," Henry teased.

Leslie laughed. "It would be good enough for me, too, if King Charles were my lover."

Henry kissed her throat. "Will nothing less than royal blood inspire you?"

She kissed his chin and whispered, "I give you leave to try."

The sun striking boldly through the porthole wakened Leslie. She sat up with a jerk and Henry reached for her sleepily.

"Oh, sir, let me go," Leslie pleaded. "It's long past sunup and the Captain'll be very angry with me. I should have taken his breakfast to him long ago. He'll have me flogged."

"He'll not have you flogged," Henry declared. "He probably thinks you've fallen overboard."

Leslie replied doubtfully. "I suppose he might." Then she said more confidently, "No one but you knows where I spent the night."

"So you may as well spend the day here, too."

"I meant to go back before morning. What'll become of me now?"

"Go back to being the cabin boy? Put those back on?" he asked incredulously, pointing to her rough shirt and pantaloons.

"They are awful," she agreed. "They scratch."

Henry stroked her shoulder and pulled her down beside him. "Those garments against skin like this? It's desecration."

"Are you suggesting that I put myself under your protection?"

"Aye, of course I am."

"And rather than wear those clothes, I'm to stay here in your cabin, naked? For the remainder of the voyage?"

Henry laughed. "Not a bad idea, that. But, no. My brother commissioned me to bring his wife some gowns and things from London. She won't mind if I give them to you, seeing your need is greater than hers."

"She'll be furious and probably scratch your eyes out. I would."

Henry climbed out of the bunk and pulled his breeches on. He opened the door.

"Stephen," he bellowed. "Stephen. Where are you, you worthless son of a strumpet?"

Stephen came down the passage at a trot. He was a plump little man of about twenty-five. He wore knee breeches and a greatcoat, in shades of brown and plainly made.

"Yes, sir. Good morning, sir. Are you ready for breakfast, sir?"

Just then he saw past Henry into the cabin and his mouth fell open in astonishment as he caught sight of Leslie.

"Breakfast for two, sir," he amended, instantly recovering his poise.

"Right, Stephen. Breakfast for two. Then bring those boxes of my sister-in-law's up here."

"Yes, sir. All of 'em?"

"All of 'em."

That evening Henry sat watching Leslie primp before his mirror. She was wearing a wonderful gown of pink satin, marvelously frilled and decorated with flounces of lace. She had done her hair in a stylish coiffure and except that her hands were roughened, she looked every inch a grand lady.

"What do you think?" she asked. "Did I alter the fit well enough?"

"Perfectly."

Leslie settled the folds of the wide skirt, caressing the satin with her fingertips. "Are you sure you want to escort me to dine with the Captain and all the fine passengers?"

"I'm sure. They'll have to know sometime where the cabin boy's got to."

"And where your concubine came from," Leslie added.

Henry got up and put on his greatcoat.

The other passengers were gathered on the deck when Henry ushered Leslie up the companionway. The moon was not yet up but the starlight and a few lanterns gave enough light to distinguish people.

Henry was about to begin introductions as people turned to stare at Leslie and her gorgeous plumage when a voice calling across the water caused everyone to turn toward the starboard rail and peer out into the darkness.

"Ahoy. Help, please help us." It was a man's voice, quavery, near at hand. "For the love of God, sir, help us."

Henry fingered the hilt of his sword. He went to the rail and called.

"Who are you?"

"English," came the answer, out of the darkness. "Our ship was wrecked in a gale and we've been adrift for nineteen days. Please, sir, we're famished for food and water."

The Captain bustled up importantly. He wore a fine greatcoat of green brocade faced with gold-colored satin and ornamented with much gold braid and lace. His tricorn hat overflowed with ostrich plumes and gold lace.

"What is the name of your ship?" called Henry.

"Stand aside, sir," ordered the Captain. "I'll handle this."

Henry shrugged cynically and moved away from the rail, back to Leslie. She put her hand in his, made uneasy by something in his manner.

The Captain called to the people in the lifeboat. "This is the Captain of the *Fair Sisters*. Who are you and why do you hail me?"

Henry felt that something about the situation was not right. He couldn't put his finger on the cause of his feeling of great danger but it was growing on him. He spoke in a low tone to Leslie. "Go below and put on your breeches and shirt. Take down your hair. Be quick."

"Why? What's…"

Henry interrupted her urgently. "Do it now."

He took her by the shoulders and turned her toward the companionway, giving her a little push. As he did so, grappling hooks whizzed upwards and caught on the port rail. Pirates swarmed over the rail and into the midst of the passengers. Leslie fled down the companionway. Henry drew his sword.

The pirates were roughly dressed; only their Captain was elegantly clad, similarly to the Captain of the *Fair Sisters*. The pirate Captain (who, in the fullness of time, would one day incarnate as Dr. Parker) was black and the pirate crew was of several nationalities and races but

128

predominantly French. It was in French that the pirate Captain shouted his orders.

The crew and passengers fought bravely. Henry engaged one of the pirates in a sword fight. As the battle raged, the moon rose and the pirate ship was revealed in silhouette, hove to some distance away.

Henry prevailed over the pirate and, as his opponent fell, found himself face-to-face with the pirate Captain. The duel was pretty evenly matched as they both sought an opening, circling and parrying. Other duels were being fought all around them and it was an English passenger who finally brought Henry down. Lunging at a pirate, the Englishman misjudged and, as the pirate side-stepped, momentum carried the Englishman forward and his sword ran deeply into Henry's side. He fell and the Captain turned to seek other prey.

Leslie came back on deck, dressed in her cabin boy's clothing. She carried a pistol in each hand and had a large knife stuck in her belt. She discharged one of the pistols point-blank into a pirate's face. He screamed and put his hands over his mangled flesh in a vain attempt to stanch the blood that streamed between his fingers. Leslie saw Henry then and ran to him.

He was conscious when she fell to her knees beside him. One of the pirates saw that he still lived and raised his cutlass to deliver the coup de grace. Leslie fired the second pistol at him and it broke his arm. He dropped the cutlass and lunged for her but Henry managed to raise his sword in time to impale the man on it. The body fell across Henry and, with the pain of his wound thus redoubled, he fainted. His head hit the deck with a nasty crack as he fell back. Leslie pulled the dying pirate off him and used her knife to slit his shirt so she could examine his wound.

The fighting was nearly over. Several pirates and many English lay on the deck, dead or wounded, the English Captain, Stephen, and Holcombe among them. The only surviving English officer looked around despairingly. Four women were among the living, huddled together near the mainmast.

"Quarter," yelled the English officer.

"You surrender?" the pirate Captain shouted back.

"We surrender and claim quarter," answered the officer.

All fighting stopped, all eyes were on the pirate Captain.

"Throw down your weapons," the Captain commanded.

The English allowed the pirates to take their weapons and the officer slowly approached the pirate Captain and offered his sword. The Captain accepted it, tossing it to one his men. "Take your men into the long boats," he ordered.

The English officer motioned for the few able-bodied sailors to help the wounded. Two of them started to pick up a wounded comrade.

"Not the wounded," the Captain said, flatly and with finality. "There's not room enough in two boats."

The English officer was aghast. "You accepted my sword."

"And you're alive. If you'd stay alive, get you into the boats."

One of the sailors went to Leslie and put a hand on her shoulder. "Come, lad."

Leslie clung to the unconscious Henry's hand. "I can't leave him."

"If you don't want to go over the side with him, you'd best come now."

"Over the side? No. They can't."

The sailor grabbed Leslie's arm and tried to drag her with him. Leslie bit him and he dropped her angrily.

"Right you are, you little fool. Stay and be damned to you."

The sailor climbed over the rail and caught a

rope, letting himself down into one of the boats. Leslie hovered protectively over Henry, watching apprehensively as the pirates threw the dead overboard, English and pirates. Then they set about throwing the wounded Englishmen over.

Leslie felt sick in body and soul as one wounded sailor begged for his life, struggling with a couple of pirates.

"No," he screamed. "No. Not over the side. Not to the sharks. Not to the sharks."

The Captain heard him and, annoyed at his noise, ran him through this his cutlass. The pirates dropped his body over the rail.

"Sniveling English coward," the Captain growled.

The English survivors started to put their women in the boats when the pirates stopped them. One of the passengers was disposed to fight but a pirate smashed him in the face with the butt of a pistol. The pirate grasped the terrified woman around the waist. She struggled and screamed for help but there was no help.

The pirate smiled at her. "Spoils of war, Madame," he told her in French.

A couple of pirates started to lift the unconscious Henry to throw him over the side. Leslie bit one who knocked her sprawling. She scrambled up with her knife in her hand, crouching to spring at him. The Captain looked at her with interest and came to see the cause of such courage in the face of impossible odds.

"Now, then," he asked in French, "what's this? Is the boy so ferocious that my pirate hearties cannot do their work?"

The bitten pirate drew his cutlass. "No, sir."

"Let him be," ordered the Captain. Then he spoke to Leslie, in English. "Do you not know the usages of war, lad?"

"Aye," Leslie answered. "I know well enough that quarter means life and these two would break your word."

"Would they now?" The Captain motioned for the two pirates to get back to work. "Find another occupation before I have you flogged for breaking my word."

They hesitated, wanting to finish with Leslie.

"God's toenails!" cried the Captain impatiently. "Get you gone!"

The two retreated from their Captain's wrath.

"Who is this," the Captain asked, gesturing at Henry, "that you're prepared to defend even at cost of your own life?"

"His name is Dr. Henry Cooper, sir. He's a physician."

The Captain used his cutlass to lay open Henry's shirt. He delicately used the point to expose his chest.

"A pretty man," the Captain remarked. "Is he your lover?"

Leslie dropped her eyes, hoping not to betray her sex. "No, sir. We're neither of us that sort."

The Captain looked at her for what seemed to Leslie a long time. He glanced back at Henry, then at his pirates. Seeing the two he wanted, he called to them. "Pulverin. Anastase. Take this Englishman to his cabin. The boy will show you which."

The two pirates picked Henry up and carried him down the companionway, with Leslie leading.

Late the next morning, Henry lay in his bunk, awake and alert. His pain had been dulled with laudanum and his wound had been bandaged. Leslie was removing the bandage to replace it when the door flew open and the Captain strode in.

"He's still alive," the Captain remarked.

The surgeon, Dr. Bramson, followed him into the room. The Captain turned to him.

"Take a look at him," he ordered, motioning the surgeon toward the bunk.

"Aye, sir," said Dr. Bramson.

Henry tried to ignore the surgeon and focused on the Captain. "Excuse me for keeping to my bunk, Captain. I'm afraid you find me at a disadvantage."

"The boy tells me you're a physician," the Captain said.

"I am."

"What do you consider your chances for survival?"

"Possibly I deceive myself, but I think I'm not to face the judgment of God just yet. Unless this headache prove fatal."

The Captain had turned aside and was looking into the open trunks and boxes. He held up the pink satin gown and looked a question at Henry.

"My wife's." answered Henry.

The Captain frowned and Leslie dared to intervene, seeing his displeasure. She looked nervously from Henry to the Captain.

"Please, sir," she said, speaking to Henry, "I haven't dared to tell you. I saw your wife go overboard during the first of the fighting last night."

Henry feigned shocked amazement then asked anxiously, "She wasn't dishonored?"

"No, sir. She died as virtuously as she lived."

Henry allowed relief to show through his simulated grief. The Captain was pleased at the news and tossed the gown back into the trunk. He addressed the surgeon.

"Well, sir? Is he like to live?"

"Aye. With care and if he's bled at judicious intervals, I believe he will, sir."

The Captain turned back to Henry. "What say you, Monsieur le Docteur?"

"God's wounds, sir, I think I've been bled enough," Henry exclaimed. "If you keep this rum-soaked incompetent away from me and leave the lad to do my bidding, I'll soon be on my feet."

The Captain nodded judicially. "And if you're let to live, will you sign the articles of the Brotherhood?"

"What choice have I?"

"None. Sign or die."

"And the lad?" asked Henry.

"He can be sent to Barbados. If so be he'll go."

Henry scowled. "Leslie? How say you?"

"I stay and sign."

Henry's feelings were mixed. For his own sake he was glad to have Leslie with him; for Leslie's sake, he wished she would go to Barbados. But he recognized that he was in no condition to enter into a contest of wills with her.

"So be it," Henry said.

The Captain abruptly strode from the cabin and the surgeon followed obsequiously. Leslie closed the door and collapsed in the chair. Henry laughed softly.

"I don't know what you're laughing for," Leslie chided him. "You're a new-made widower."

"Wedded and widowed, all in the space of a minute. And never bedded at all."

"I mistrust the Captain. I'm afraid you'll have to defend your virtue once your life is safe."

"How so?"

"As you lay on the deck last night, he called you a pretty man. It was after he admired your chest that he decided to grant you quarter."

"The Devil he did."

The door flew open again and Leslie quickly assumed a more servant-like demeanor. A couple of pirates came in, picked up one of the chests and left. Others came for the other chests. Two of them slung Henry in a blanket and carried him out.

"Leslie," Henry cried, "bring the medicine chest!"

She scurried to close the chest and hasten after the men.

The pirates transferred Henry to their own ship, the *Adamant*, permitting Leslie to trail along. Henry's wound was painful and he slept much of the time during the two days that it took the ship to reach its island destination. They set up camp on a wide white beach with low slopes, very green, stretching back into the interior. Palm trees fringed the beach.

The sailors erected awnings for shade and piled their booty and supplies at random. Leslie kept the medicine chest in her own hands despite the pirates' interest in it. Henry's wound had opened in the move from the ship and Leslie knelt beside him, trying to stanch the flow of blood.

"Leslie, is my medicine chest here?" Henry gasped through his pain.

"Aye. Shall I get some laudanum for you?"

"No. Find my box and get some linen to make a bandage. Then get me a bottle of rum."

"Rum? Should you drink rum in your condition?"

"God's teeth and toenails! I'll do the prescribing."

"Aye, sir," Leslie said, still doubting the wisdom of drinking rum with an open wound in one's side but more afraid of the effect on her patient if she opposed him. She went to a pile of trunks and boxes and opened one. Taking out a linen nightgown, she went back to Henry. Kneeling beside him, she used her knife to nick the fabric so she could tear it into strips. She folded one of the strips into a pad and placed it over the wound, holding it there.

"That garment was none of mine," Henry

remarked.

"No, sir. I believe it was Mister Holcombe's."

"Ah, yes, Holcombe. What's become of him? I haven't seen him about."

"He went over the side that night."

Henry put his hand on the linen pad. "I'll hold it in place," he said. "You fetch me the rum."

"Aye, sir." Unwillingly, Leslie went to get the rum.

Henry was interested to see some pirates go past, carrying a couple of wild pigs they had killed. They dug pits and gathered firewood for the barbecue.

That night, under the tropic moon, the pirates had a fandango to celebrate the taking of the *Fair Sisters*. They built a huge bonfire and drank and fought and sang and danced, as their individual fancies took them. Henry was unable to leave his pallet under the awning and Leslie sat with him, watching the action. The Captain danced a minuet with Pulverin, to the accompaniment of a guitar. But the minuet was too genteel and stately for their feelings.

"Play something more sprightly," the Captain shouted to the guitarist.

He switched abruptly to a fast-paced ditty and the Captain and some of the others danced a jig. Leslie bounced to her feet and began to dance.

"Don't you love to dance?" she cried, carried away in the joy of the music.

"Dancing is well enough," Henry agreed. "It's the music I can't abide."

Leslie dropped to her knees beside him. "You don't like music?" she asked incredulously. "How...Oh, I see. You don't like this man's music. I grant you he's not the best, still he's..."

Henry interrupted testily. "No, I mean I can't abide any music. Ugly, screeching noises. It gets on my nerves."

"Oh, how much you miss," Leslie commiserated.

The Captain left off dancing and strode over to Henry. Leslie stepped back, into the shadows.

"You seem much better tonight, Monsieur le Docteur."

"It's true enough, sir. Tomorrow I shall essay to walk across the beach to bathe in the sea."

"Swim, you mean?"

"Aye. There's nothing like exercise to take the stiffness out of the body."

"I don't believe in sailors learning to swim," the Captain declared. "It only prolongs the suffering when they're forced into the sea. I've always thanked the good God above that I don't know how myself."

"You speak as if that were every sailor's

inevitable end."

"Better the sea then the gallows."

"Better one's own bed of natural causes. At the end of a long and lusty life," smiled Henry.

"Perhaps. I prefer my bed for other uses than to die in. And I know how to be patient. A very good night to you, Monsieur le Docteur."

The Captain strode away, back to the fandango, leaving Henry to look after him, bemused, and Leslie to scowl after him from the shadows.

Not many days after the fandango, the pirates finished careening the *Adamant*. They were working at righting the ship after hauling it over to expose the bottom, one side at a time, to scrape off the barnacles and seaweed and repair the damage of worms. Henry was well enough to walk but still very weak and in a great deal of pain. Leslie helped him to stand and, gritting his teeth against the pain and leaning on the girl, Henry went across the sand to the sea. At the edge of the water, he stripped and waded out to where the sea could support his weight. Leslie stood at the water's edge and watched anxiously. Henry lay back in the water, floating serenely, his eyes closed against the dazzle of the sun on the sparkling blue Caribbean. Presently, he rolled over, opening his eyes, and swam a few strokes

141

out to sea. He let the surf carry him back to the beach.

Some days later, Pulverin came to Leslie and announced that they would load the ship and depart the next day. He inquired after Henry's wound, remarking that it was apparently healed. Leslie feared the Captain's response to a report of Henry's wellness so she pulled as long a face as she could and hinted darkly at some vague but pervasive lack of health in the good doctor.

At first light the pirates broke camp. They packed everything into boxes and trunks and carried them on board. Henry was almost completely healed, his wound requiring only a small bandage, and he could move with nearly his normal ease and grace. Leslie held his greatcoat but he declined to wear it.

"Where are we bound for now?" Leslie asked, folding the coat.

"Cap Francais. The Captain will sell the *Fair Sisters* there and outfit for another voyage."

"Do you suppose we can escape at Cap Francais?"

"Why, Leslie, we've signed on as Brethren of the Coast. Have you lost your taste for pirating before you've even indulged it?"

"Aye. I've had enough of the sea, pirate or no."

"The Captain very handsomely offered to set you ashore at Barbados."

"I'll not desert you, sir."

"My wound is nearly healed. I don't want you to stay against your own wishes."

His obtuseness irritated Leslie. "The trouble with educated men is that they talk too much. It's time we were aboard the ship."

Henry cast her a quizzical look then led the way across the beach and up the gangplank. Leslie followed at a decorous distance with the medicine chest.

The trip from the nameless little island to Cap Francais was quickly accomplished. As the *Adamant* came into sight of the French port, Henry stood on deck, leaning against the rail, watching a flight of seabirds. The birds swooped and swirled in the sky, making Henry wonder if there was purpose to the aerobatics or if they flew for mere enjoyment. The Captain came to stand beside him. He also watched the birds for a few minutes in silence. At last he looked at Henry and spoke.

"I have a home in Cap Francais. It would give me great pleasure if you'd be my guest during our stay."

"A home?" Henry was unable to keep his surprise out of his voice.

The Captain was amused. "It surprises you that a pirate should own a home? But we don't always live on our vessels. When we divide the prize money, the men will drink and whore until they're broke and then we'll put to sea in search of other prey. Until then, I'm a respected citizen of Cap Francais."

Henry had had time to gather his wits. "Thank you, sir, I'd be most happy to accept your hospitality."

The two men bowed formally to one another and the Captain went back to the quarterdeck.

Henry's fears for Leslie knew no bounds as they disembarked on the quay. Anastase led the way through the shouting, bustling crowd: pirates, merchants, townspeople, French, English, Spanish, African, Italian, Indian. It seemed to Henry and Leslie that there were people of every race and nationality, dressed in every costume imaginable. Fabrics of every hue and pattern known to humanity adorned the people on the quay. Henry tried to assume the demeanor of a traveled Englishman but Leslie frankly gawked. She hurried after Henry and Anastase, carrying the medicine chest, afraid of being left behind in the tumult of this strange place.

A few streets from the quay, the town turned staid and calm. The buildings were homes instead

144

of businesses and the few people on the street were mostly servants or housewives, intent on homely errands. Anastase led them up a hill and turned in at a wrought iron gate. He took them up the walk, through gardens of beautiful blossoms, few of which were known to either Henry or Leslie. The mansion at the end of the walk was built of stone, with a balcony that ran the width of the house. Anastase knocked on the door and it was opened by a lovely young quadroon girl, twelve years old, exquisitely gowned in pale blue silk.

"Anastase," she exclaimed, smiling happily. "My father is at the quay?" she asked in French.

"Oui," Anastase answered. "He has bid me tell you that all is well and he will see you tomorrow. The business is apt to detain him until late, you understand. In the meantime, he has sent this gentleman and bids you welcome him." He turned to Henry and spoke in English, "Mademoiselle Violette is the Captain's daughter."

Henry bowed deeply and smiled gravely. "Enchante, mademoiselle. Dr. Henry Cooper, at your service."

Violette gave him a shy smile and her hand. He kissed it gallantly and she stepped back. He followed her inside and Leslie started to follow but Anastase took her arm and jerked her back.

He muttered something in French and pulled her around to the rear and entered the kitchen door without knocking.

Matilde and Yvonne looked up from their baking, startled as Anastase and Leslie barged into the kitchen. The maids were young and pretty and not averse to a bit of flirtatious banter to enliven a monotonous day. Neither spoke any English so their conversation was entirely in French, some of which Leslie could guess at with fair accuracy, some of which left her puzzled.

"Anastase," cried Matilde. "So the Captain is home."

"Oui, the Captain is home. He has sent a guest to Mademoiselle. You'd better send old Marguerite to them and tell her not to leave the Englishman alone with Mademoiselle Violette."

"An Englishman?" exclaimed Yvonne with horror. "In this house?"

"Do not be afraid, little one," Anastase reassured her. "He is not an ugly demon as you've been led to suppose. He's just a man and a member of the Brethren so there's nothing to fear."

Matilde spoke seriously, "Oh, if he's a member of the Brethren, it's all right."

Anastase pointed to Leslie. "This is his servant. Be nice to him and perhaps he'll be nice to you."

Grinning impishly, Anastase made his escape as the two maids took umbrage at his implication.

Yvonne approached Leslie with some trepidation. "Are you also an Englishman?"

Leslie judged it best to appear at her ease and assumed an air of confidence and command that she was far from feeling. "Aye. English. And hungry and thirsty. Fetch me food and punch." She mimed eating and drinking.

Yvonne understood and went to the cupboard to assemble a meal for her, taking down bread and cold meat.

"You'd better rout out old Marguerite first," Matilde told her, rolling out pastry.

"Lord, yes," said Yvonne, setting a bowl on the table, "before that poor child dies of fright. I wonder what the Englishman really does look like?"

Catching the word "English" again, Leslie guessed that the maids were discussing Henry curiously.

"The Englishman is ugly as sin," she said. "He's old and diseased and he's got a wart on his chin this big." She mimed old and screwed her face up to indicate ugly. She held her fingers to indicate a very large wart and pointed to her chin, wrinkling her nose in distaste.

147

"Time out of mind," she confided, "I've thanked God that I'm not a comely young wench. You've no idea of his loathsomeness."

Matilde stared wide-eyed at Leslie and Yvonne dashed to the door.

In the parlor, Henry was sitting on the high-backed, plum-colored sofa, leaning a little toward the other end of it and looking down. Yvonne burst through a door and saw Henry from the back. Leaping to the conclusion that Violette was the object of his attention, she shrieked. Henry turned an amazed look on her and Violette came from an alcove at the opposite end of the room, carrying the book she'd gone to find.

Very much surprised at Yvonne's behavior, she hurried to her. "Yvonne, what is it? What has happened?"

"Where is the Englishman? Are you all right? The Englishman's servant said…"

Yvonne faltered to a stop.

"Said what?" demanded Violette. "What's the matter with you?"

It dawned on Yvonne that this Englishman was neither old nor ugly and that he was before her. In confusion she backed toward the door. "Nothing. I beg your pardon, mademoiselle. And monsieur. I will send Marguerite to you."

"There is no necessity. Monsieur has asked to

be shown his room as he is somewhat fatigued with his recent wound. Show him to the Primrose Chamber, Yvonne."

Henry rose and picked up the book he'd been studying. Violette handed him the book she held. He bowed to the little mademoiselle and turned toward Yvonne.

The servant curtseyed to Violette. "Yes, mademoiselle."

Nervously, she led Henry out of the parlor and up the grand staircase. He followed her down a long corridor.

"What exactly did my servant say to you?" Henry asked in French.

"It was nothing, monsieur. I see now that he was having a joke with me."

"Tell me what he said. I'm fond of a joke."

"Oh, monsieur, it was nothing at all."

Henry took her arm and stopped her, turning her to face him. "Yvonne, you are not my servant, but I have given you an order. I expect to be obeyed."

"He does not speak French, monsieur, and so he used the gestures to communicate. I think I must have misunderstood him. I thought he meant that you would not be good for the little Mademoiselle Violette to know."

"Did you? Well, I think you probably understood him very well, Yvonne. He is an impudent rascal. Thank you. Now, which of these doors belongs to the Primrose Chamber?"

She opened a door and stepped back. "This one, monsieur."

The room was sumptuous. The bed was hung with primrose curtains and mosquito netting. The floor was of glazed tile of primrose and green. The windows overlooked the town and the quay, giving a fine view of the Caribbean in the distance, roofed over with towering billows of white cloud formations.

Henry looked around appreciatively. "I wish to bathe. Send up the tub and much hot water. And send my baggage up right away."

"Oui, monsieur. Will you dine with mademoiselle?"

"I think not. Send some fruit and wine up. And a dish of roast fowl."

"Oui, monsieur." Yvonne started out of the room.

"And send my servant to me."

Yvonne was much relieved that the mischievous Leslie would be removed from the kitchen. With a final, "Oui, monsieur," she went out, closing the door behind her.

Knowing it might be their one night together for a long time to come, Henry and Leslie made the most of it. The remains of the meal were still on the table as he sat watching her luxuriate in the bath. He wore only a linen towel around his hips. She had washed her hair and it gleamed in the candlelight.

"It's wonderful to be clean again," she murmured. "And my own sex."

"It's wonderful to see you out of those cabin boy's clothes. I'll give you some money and tomorrow you can at least buy some better ones."

He picked up another linen towel and went to put his hand in the water.

"Your bath is nearly cold," he said.

"Aye. You'll have to rub some warmth back into me."

She stood up and Henry wrapped the towel around her. She put her arms around his neck and kissed him.

The next morning Henry walked down to the quay and boarded the *Adamant*. The Captain was sharing out the prize money to his crew. He looked up and saw Henry.

"Ah, Monsieur le Docteur. Have you come to see how well the articles of the Brethren of the Coast function?"

Henry greeted the Captain and leaned against the mainmast to watch as each man received his share. Those who'd been wounded were paid extra, according to the schedule of benefits contained in the articles.

"Together with the compensation for losing his right hand, that completes the share of Pierre le Nez Gros," the Captain announced.

One of the pirates spoke up, "I'll hold it for him until he's well."

There was a lot of laughter at the offer.

The Captain smiled and said dryly, "That is very kind of you, but I think I will myself hold it for him." He put the coins in a small bag and put the bag in his money chest, which still held considerable golden coins. He rose, closing the lid of the chest. "And that completes the sharing out. Emile, pick two men and form a watch. When that's done, the rest of you may disembark."

A great shout of happy anticipation went up. The Captain had two men carry the chest down the companionway. He followed and signaled for Henry to come along. When the chest had been stowed in his cabin and the two sailors were gone, the Captain set out a cut glass decanter of wine and two cut glass goblets. He gestured at one of the chairs drawn up to the table.

"Be seated, Monsieur le Docteur. You will join me in a glass of Madeira?"

"With pleasure, Mon Capitaine."

The noise of the departing crew gradually died

away. The Captain poured the wine and they sat down at the table.

Henry lifted his glass and toasted the Captain. "To your continued prosperity, sir."

The Captain made acknowledgement and offered a toast to Henry. "And to your continued good health. You are quite recovered now?"

"Perfectly."

The Captain gazed at him with what began to look like amorous intent. Henry started to feel uncomfortable and wondered if Leslie could possibly be right that the Captain had designs on his virtue, such as it was.

"How soon do we put to sea again?" Henry asked.

"It will take those rascals nearly a week to spend their prize money. When that's done, we'll seek another, richer prize. Your countrymen are notoriously poor. Next time we'll look for a rich Spanish galleon."

The Captain unbuttoned his greatcoat.

"And where will you set the ambuscade? There is a sea lane the Spanish treasure ships use, is there not?"

The Captain rose. "There is."

He came around the table and sat on Henry's lap. Henry spilled his wine. The Captain took the glass from his hand and placed the hand inside his waistcoat.

"Monsieur le Capitaine," began Henry, "you mistake me…" The truth seeped through his hand to his head. "Oh. Oh, another?"

"It surprises me that you haven't penetrated my disguise before this."

"A fault of my imagination. Which shall be righted at once."

The Captain shrugged off her greatcoat and unbuttoned her waistcoat, revealing a very feminine torso under her linen shirt. She divested Henry of his greatcoat.

That night Henry dined with the Captain and Violette at the mansion on the hill. The Captain sat at the head of the table with Henry on her right and Violette on her left. The girl was daintily dressed in a gown of rosy silk and wore luscious pink tropical flowers in her hair; Henry wore a black brocade greatcoat embroidered all over with silver and a shirt of wonderful ruffles and lace that the Captain had provided for him. She was gowned in fuchsia silk, low cut, with diamonds flashing at her throat and ears. The fire of rubies and emeralds, diamonds and sapphires glinted with every movement of her hands. Her hair was dressed high in the French fashion with yet more gems interwoven.

Yvonne brought in a platter on which reposed a roasted peacock, adorned with his own feathers in a great fan, his beak gilded, and ingeniously propped up to imitate the living bird.

"Peacock feathers!" snorted the Captain. "What nonsense is this?"

Violette giggled. "Oh, Papa, it's the latest fashion. You know the nobles in France dine like this every night of their lives."

"On feathers?" She smiled at Violette. "Oh, well, if it's the fashion."

She removed the feathers, setting them on a plate Yvonne held for her. Then she carved the bird and Yvonne passed dishes of rice and vegetables. She went to the sideboard for a bottle of wine and filled the glasses.

"Violette," the Captain said, "my little one, how do your studies progress?"

"I'm doing excellently well in geography and grammar. Somewhat less well in Latin, worse still in Greek, but very well in arithmetic. Oh, Papa, mayn't I study astronomy and algebra? I would so like to know how to navigate."

"And run away to sea? Never. I've told you again and again, you shall be a fine lady. I have in mind a brilliant match for you."

"But, Papa…"

"That's enough, Violette."

Recognizing the tone of finality, Violette desisted. But she was a young lady of spirit and felt she must at least tease her mother a bit. "Well, perhaps I shan't mind so much if you choose a handsome Englishman for me."

The Captain ignored her and smiled at Henry. "Her youth must be her excuse, Monsieur le Docteur."

"Think nothing of it, mon Capitaine; I have young cousins and they are frequently naughty in a similar vein."

"You are most gracious."

"She is a charming child," Henry said, dividing a smile between the two. "I find myself somewhat at a loss, though. Would it be impertinent to ask who her…mother…is?"

"Most impertinent. However, I suppose it sounds odd to you. I taught her to call me Papa before I was as well established as I am now, to prevent betrayal by childish lips. Now we're used to it and it persists. As to your real question, who is her father…" The Captain reached out to hold her daughter's hand for a moment. "My husband was captain of a French man-of-war. We sailed from St. Malo thirteen years ago."

"He was killed?"

"My father died bravely, Monsieur le Docteur," Violette told him proudly. "Protecting

156

me and my mother from the Spaniards. Of course, I was not, in truth, yet born."

"Violette was born five months later, here in Cap Francais. My husband's defense gave me time to get into the longboat with some sailors. I saw my husband fall as we pushed off."

"Why did you return to the sea?" Henry asked, seeing that his curiosity was not resented.

"There are not many ways for a woman to obtain a competence," Violette explained seriously. "And the women of my family are never whores."

The Captain took up the tale. "I have little taste for serving and, anyway, I wanted to make life secure for Violette. There is little chance to earn a fortune by honest means so I determined to become a pirate. By the time the others penetrated my disguise, I had performed my duties well enough to have won their respect. I neutered one pig of a first mate who would have dishonored me and that brought still more respect. It wasn't long before I had my own ship."

Henry raised his glass. "To a gallant lady."

A couple of weeks later, the Captain was in a mood to enjoy her femininity, as she stood at the window of her chamber, looking through the bright moonlight at the harbor. A silk and ivory fan was in her hand and she used it languidly.

Henry sat in a chair across the room and watched her. She turned from the window and walked toward him, the fan held coquettishly so she could look at him over the top of it.

"This will be our last night ashore for some time," she remarked. She forgot to manage her skirts and kicked at them pettishly. "God's ears and eyeballs, how I hate these gowns. Always getting bunched up between one's legs. Why women wear them is beyond my comprehension. Here, help me unfasten these hooks."

Henry laughed and complied, kissing her bare shoulders as he unhooked the bodice. "Women wear them because men like them," he murmured. "Even you, mon Capitaine."

She turned in his arms and kissed him passionately. Then she left his embrace to take the gown off, leaving herself in a swirl of petticoats.

"We sail in the morning?" Henry inquired, doffing his greatcoat.

"Aye. And I'll be glad enough to get the quarterdeck under my feet again. If it weren't for Violette, I'd never come ashore at all."

"Do you always carry a strumpet with you? Or am I the first?"

The Captain looked at him steadily. "I wondered if you'd worked that out. You're quite intelligent."

"Yes, I know," Henry replied. "Will you answer my question?"

"The crew won't realize, you know. They'll think you're just the physician. I've arranged for the surgeon to sail on Steubers' rotten old tub."

"Do you think your crew is composed entirely of idiots?" Henry asked dryly.

"Well, what does it matter? I'm the captain and it's no wonderful thing for the captain to carry his pleasure with him to sea."

"And what of me?" he demanded. "Suppose I don't care to play the role you've cast for me?"

The Captain laughed. "God's teeth and toenails, monsieur. You speak as if you'd a choice. You still have only me or the gallows to choose between."

They looked deeply into one another's eyes and the Captain spoke softly. "Is the choice so very difficult?"

"No," he answered. "It's not a difficult choice at all."

The days on board the *Adamant* were relatively pleasant. The sea and sky were unceasingly lovely and the clouds were an ever-changing source of fascination. Leslie returned to her role of cabin boy. Henry began to learn the workings of the ship and the strategy of the

Captain. He marveled at her command of the pirate crew and her grasp of the tactics of sea warfare. She kept the ship hidden among the islands along the Spanish Main, waiting and watching for a treasure ship. They mostly traveled in company, for safety, but she knew that with patience she would find one alone, possibly crippled.

One afternoon the lookout spotted a galleon sailing by itself. The Captain took out her glass and watched it for some time, wary of cunning Spanish traps. Many Spanish ships had been taken in the past few years and she knew the Spaniards were anxious to clear the sea lanes of pirates. When she was satisfied, she gave her orders.

The Captain caused the Spanish galleon to collide with the *Adamant* broadside. The galleon's bowsprit was caught in the rigging of the pirate ship and the two vessels were locked together. As Henry watched, the Captain lowered her cutlass sharply and the cannoneers fired a broadside into the galleon. Caught as she was, the Spanish ship could answer only with musketry.

The Captain led the pirates over the bowsprit to the deck of the galleon. Henry was among the first to board. The Spaniards fought hard but were overpowered. Leslie had been told to stay on the *Adamant* until Henry signaled to her to bring the case of surgical knives and saws – necessary to a ship's doctor even though he was not a surgeon.

Henry fought alongside the other pirates until he saw that the fight was won. Then he sheathed his sword and signaled to Leslie and began to tend the wounded pirates, stanching their bleeding and bandaging their wounds. Leslie assisted as best she could. Henry knelt beside an unconscious pirate whose leg was badly mauled.

"This poor devil's got to have this leg off. Leslie, get someone to help you hold him in case he wakes while I'm operating."

Anastase was nearby and Leslie took his arm and tugged him toward the wounded man. He saw the necessity and called another man to come and help. The two held the wounded man firmly while Henry cut and sawed, tying off the great blood vessels. Leslie handed him implements and bandages and threw the severed leg overboard.

As they worked, the Spanish captain surrendered. Henry ignored the activity around him as the Spanish survivors who were whole were herded into the longboats and those who were not were thrown over the side. He and Leslie worked to save the lives of those who could be helped. When they had all been moved to the pirate ship, he sent Leslie below, then moved among them, making them as comfortable as he could with rum or laudanum.

Leslie was sitting up in his bunk when Henry finally went to his cabin. He locked the door behind him and stripped to the waist to wash the blood from his arms and chest and face.

"Will they live?" Leslie asked.

"Most of them. I doubt if the leg amputee survives, though."

He toweled himself dry and climbed into the bunk. He took Leslie in his arms, seeking comfort after the twin horrors of battle and surgery.

"What will happen to me when you've got me with child?" Leslie asked softly.

"I'll buy you a house in Cap Francais and you can stay ashore – retire from the sea. Why, has the time come so soon?"

"Not yet. Please God, it never will."

"That would please me as well. I've no wish for a bastard brood."

They kissed and in the intensity of the moment, failed to hear the movement of the door handle.

The Captain, dressed in fresh clothing, sought to celebrate her victory. Finding Henry's door locked, she raised her foot and kicked until the lock splintered out of the wood. The door flew open to show her Henry and Leslie in each other's arms, looking at her with amazement. Henry began to laugh. He got out of the bunk and pulled on his breeches. He tossed her shirt and breeches to Leslie. She dressed, keeping herself well covered from the Captain's furious gaze.

"God's wounds, monsieur," the Captain raged, "I don't find the fun in this. The cabin boy?"

Henry could hardly speak for laughing. "I never thought to put horns on a woman. Nothing's ever as one expects, is it?"

"I'm damned if I'll be made a laughingstock by my own strumpet," the Captain snarled, drawing her cutlass. Henry yanked his sword from the scabbard that hung from the back of a chair. They fenced up the companionway and onto the deck.

"To the rail, Leslie," Henry shouted. "We'll have to chance the sharks."

He fought with desperation, the Captain with all the energy of a woman betrayed and enraged. A couple of the crew made movement to interfere but she waved them back.

"Let be," she grated. "He's mine."

When Leslie made it to the rail, Henry threw his sword away and grabbed her hand. Together they leaped over the rail and into the water.

"Shall we lower the longboat, Monsieur le Capitaine?" Pulverin asked.

"No," the Captain said, sheathing her cutlass.

"Let the sharks have them."

Henry and Leslie swam toward a small island. They were nearly to the beach when exhaustion overtook Leslie. Henry saw that her strength was flagging.

"Come, Leslie,' he said. 'It's only a little farther. See, the beach is right here."

"I can't," she panted. "I can't."

She sank under the rippling waves and Henry pulled her to the surface, although his own stamina was nearly exhausted.

"Fight, Leslie. You mustn't give up now. We'll be safe in a few minutes."

"I'm sorry," she gasped, and slipped under the surface again.

Henry pulled her up into the air. "Rest, then. Relax and let the sea float your body."

But Leslie was too worn out even to listen. Twice more the water closed over her head; twice more Henry dragged her back. The third time he had not the strength. Leslie sank into the blue waters of the Caribbean.

Henry wanted to go under with her but the instinct for survival was too strong for him. He struggled on toward the island and after what seemed hours, found himself rolling in the sandy breakers. He used the last of his strength to pull himself onto the dry sand and lay there, stunned with grief.

Hearing a noise, he raised his head and saw five Indian men coming down the beach toward him. They wore only loincloths and feather head-dresses. Their only weapons were clubs. He tried to rise and had managed to get to his knees when the Indians formed a semi-circle around him. Without a word being spoken, the man in the center raised his club and brought it down on Henry's head. His last coherent thought was a confused gratitude that the Indians had sent him to rejoin Leslie.

PART IV

Woman's Greatest Adventure

Dr. Parker was sitting next to Pat Mayhew, who was lying back in the recliner in her office, deeply in a trance. She was rapidly taking notes as the tape recorder beside her transcribed the session.

"Why are you angry?" she asked.

"Because I have no children. My husband is sad about that." Pat answered, his demeanor one of impatience and controlled anger.

"Your husband? You're a young matron, then?"

"Not so very young. It has always been my dearest wish to have children."

"But you can't? What is your name, by the way?"

"White Water Woman, because once I fell into the rapids and nearly drowned."

"I see." Dr. Parker hesitated, then plunged forward. "Why can't you have children?"

"My husband is incapable. Impotent."

"What tribe do you belong to?"

"Absoroka. The people you call Crow."

"Do you know the year?"

"1823. The white men, the men who come to

trap beaver in our streams call it 1823."

"If you're dissatisfied with your husband, why don't you divorce him? Your tribal laws allow that, do they not?"

"Yes," Pat answered reluctantly. "But it's not Killer of Bears' fault. He feels badly enough about it already."

"Are you in love with him?"

"No, not exactly in love with him. But he loves me and I have a great affection for him. And I have pity, also."

"Where do you live?"

"We're camped on a creek in Absoroka – you call it Wyoming. Yellowstone Park. The men are hunting buffalo out on the prairie."

"Are there many white men in your country, living among you?"

"There are a few white men. In the mountains, mostly. Right now there are two with our hunters. Only one of them is black. I cannot understand why one of the white men is black. He wears Indian clothes, but in all other respects, he is white. Except his skin – it glistens in the sun. He is very handsome."

"Does he talk to you?"

That shocked the respectable matron that Pat had been. "Oh, no. That wouldn't be proper. Sometimes my husband invites him to eat with us, though. I like him."

"Do these white men live with you permanently?"

"No, these two just stopped to visit and hunt with us a few days. They trap in the beaver streams in the mountains."

"I see. Tell me what you are doing now."

Pat began to describe the Indian encampment. There were thirteen Crow families so there were thirteen tipis; all faced east and all were decorated with paintings. The women were going about their business, scraping buffalo hides they had pegged out on the ground, putting the meat on racks to dry, and caring for the children.

The younger children were playing, joined by the dogs and puppies. The older girls were helping the women while the older boys were being instructed in marksmanship with their bows by a couple of old men.

White Water Woman, Ripe Corn Woman, and Squash Blossom Woman sat near one of the tipis, slicing buffalo meat into thin strips. A cradleboard, containing an infant, leaned against the tipi next to Ripe Corn Woman. It was fringed and embroidered with porcupine quill beads. The women wore deerskin dresses that reached to their calves and were decorated with fringing and quill beads, as well as with dentalium and elk teeth.

169

They wore moccasins with designs of quill beads and jewelry of shells and beads. They all wore their hair in long braids intertwined with feathers and finished at the ends with disks of abalone shell.

"When my second son was born," said Ripe Corn Woman, "the midwife said she'd never seen so much blood. She really feared that I would bleed to death."

"My babies come easily," Squash Blossom Woman said complacently. "I've never had anything that could be called complications. The women in my family always bear their children quickly and without trouble."

"I was in labor with my first for three days. It's a miracle we both lived. The midwife said she'd never seen a baby born alive after such a prolonged labor."

"Now, with my first, I began to go into labor as I was cooking supper. And she was born before sunrise. Well before sunrise."

"Well, it's a great boon to be able to have children without long drawn out suffering," sighed Ripe Corn Woman. "It leaves one so weak and..." She was interrupted by the infant, who had awakened and begun to cry. She took the baby out of the cradleboard and adjusted her dress to allow the child to nurse. White Water Woman

got up and walked away, tired of having no exper-
iences of her own to offer, tired of seeing the
other women with happiness that was denied her.

Squash Blossom Woman shook her head. "It's
a shame she's barren, she loves children so
much."

"Spotted Lily Woman says it's not White
Water Woman's fault, but Killer of Bears who is
incapable."

"Is that right? Well, she should know. Being
his sister, White Water Woman would have
confided in her, I suppose."

"I don't know that she loves children so
much," Ripe Corn Woman mused thoughtfully.
"She could divorce Killer of Bears."

"Or take a lover. That white man – the black
one – have you noticed how his eyes follow her
wherever she goes?"

"Squash Blossom Woman! Oh, do you think
she might?"

"Well, I've seen her look at him…" she trailed
off, looking at Ripe Corn Woman significantly.

"That reminds me. You know that Fog Rolling
over the Grass is camped with his people on the
Elk River?"

Squash Blossom Woman nodded.

"Woman Who Limps told me that the day they
pitched camp there, Fog Rolling over the Grass

171

found that his wife had been carrying on with his cousin. And when he beat her, the cousin interfered and now the cousin has been banished from the camp. Did you ever hear anything to equal that?"

The women were pleasurably horrified by the magnitude of their gossip fodder.

"Which wife is that?" asked Squash Blossom Woman. "Beaded Necklace Woman or Antelope Woman?"

"Antelope Woman. She was a captive, you know. Sioux."

"I remember. He took her when Buffalo Hump led that war party into the Sioux country three winters ago."

"She's been nothing but trouble ever since. Perhaps she'll run away with the cousin."

Ripe Corn Woman laughed. "Probably Fog Rolling over the Grass hopes so."

Squash Blossom Woman laughed as she rose to her feet. "I must go and hang this meat to dry." She took a basketful of meat strips to the drying rack.

White Water Woman went to her tipi and collected her riding gear – a feathered and beaded quirt, saddle and blanket, and hackamore with reins. She left the camp and walked out to the horse herd. She put everything but the hackamore

172

and reins on the ground and stood watching the horses for a few minutes. Having located her little appaloosa mare, Walks Like a Cougar, she threw the hackamore and reins over her shoulder, walked toward her, clicking her tongue and holding out her hand with a few berries in it.

The little mare hadn't been ridden for a few days and was a little skittish. She danced as White Water Woman went closer to her, then, as the woman was nearly close enough for the mare to eat the berries, she snorted and danced away. She trotted toward some trees a little distance away, looking back to see if White Water Woman was following. She smiled and stood still, holding out the berries. Another mare came up to her, neck outstretched to sniff at the berries. White Water Woman closed her hand and lowered it, then stroked the mare's neck with her free hand. Walks Like a Cougar came trotting over, tossing her head and whickering. White Water Woman laughed and the other mare moved away, nibbling at the grass as she went.

The little appaloosa slowed to a walk and White Water Woman held out the berries again. The mare sidled up to her and delicately took the berries, lipping them into her mouth. The woman murmured endearments, stroking the mare's face and neck. Walks Like a Cougar gently rubbed her

173

jaw on White Water Woman's shoulder. She slipped the hackamore on the mare, adjusting it so it wouldn't fret her. She led the mare over to the saddle and finished tacking up. All the time she worked, she told the mare how lovely she was and how swiftly she ran and how perfect she was in every way. The mare stood quietly, only pawing a little with one forefoot to show how eager she was for a gallop over the prairie. White Water Woman drew up the cinch and tucked the end of the strap in. She put a foot in the stirrup and lifted herself easily into the saddle. The little appaloosa hardly waited until she was firmly seated before she began to run.

White Water Woman grasped the reins but let the mare set her own pace. She ran past the encampment, out onto the prairie. The woman clung with her knees and exulted in the speed and excitement of racing her shadow across the rippling grassland. Not wanting Walks Like a Cougar to exhaust herself, White Water Woman squeezed her lower legs into the mare's barrel, signaling her to slacken speed. She brought the horse to a trot and then to a walk. They went back past the camp and up into the hills.

The mare splashed through a little creek and went past some cottonwoods, just turning their fall colors, up into the pines. The serene beauty all around them brought both horse and rider into harmony with the tranquility of the forest. A doe with two fawns looked at White Water Woman and Walks Like a Cougar with mild curiosity before she calmly led her babies away. The creek, shallow and clear, ran swiftly down the hill. The light and shade played tag over the water, now highlighting the varicolored pebbles on its bottom, now investing its curves and hollows with mystery.

White Water Woman dismounted at a little falls and stood for a few minutes watching the creek tumble down a shady, fern-covered miniature ravine. The water was white and smoky-looking as it fell and splashed. She knew the myths and stories about the waterfall and was thinking of them as she stood there. The mare had run her energy down to a reasonable level so she dropped the reins, knowing the horse wouldn't stray far before stepping on them and stopping herself.

Both drank deeply from the pool of cold, clear water. The mare cropped the grass in the little clearing; the woman slipped off her dress and submerged herself in the pool, gasping at the first touch of the icy water. Then she swam about, enjoying the silence and the serenity. She felt her body numbing with the cold and swam under the

175

falling water to rouse herself.

She climbed out of the pool and stood in a patch of sunshine, using her hands to wipe the water away. Walks Like a Cougar came over and nuzzled her arm. She held out her empty hands to show the mare that she had no more berries. The horse whickered and went back to cropping grass.

White Water Woman wasn't dry but she was no longer soaking wet so she put on her clothes and caught up the reins. She mounted and rode back to the camp at a sedate walk. Far out on the prairie she could see little specks moving in and out of a cloud of dust. She knew that they were the hunters and the buffalo and that the black white man was with them.

Hezekiah Stern, who would one day, in another life, be known as Dr. Parker, had been in the mountains for nearly half his thirty-one years. He had run away from the Missouri blacksmith who was his master and joined a fur trapping brigade when he was seventeen. Life in the mountains was hard and not many lived to a ripe old age but it was a great improvement over the old life. Here he was his own man, made his own decisions, suffered or rejoiced as the result might be. And he called no man sir unless of his own volition.

Hezekiah had hunted buffalo with various

176

bands of Indians many times. He knew how to drive the buffalo into a compacted mass and turn them so they ran in a circle, then to ride with the others around them, shooting into the mass to bring down the meat. The Indians were mostly using bows and arrows but Hezekiah and his white friend were using muskets. For this kind of work, the Indians were far more efficient. They could accurately fire an incredible number of arrows while each man loaded his musket, fired and reloaded.

When as many buffalo as could be butchered that afternoon were down, the Indians stopped killing and allowed the rest to escape. First they removed the livers, sprinkled them with gall, and ate them raw, warm from the carcasses. Hezekiah worked with them, dressing and skinning the beasts, then wrapping the meat in the skins and placing it on the travois. He straightened to ease his back muscles and noticed that the clouds had begun to drift across the sun in increasing numbers. When next he noticed, the sky was overcast and it smelled like rain.

As they neared the camp, the women and children and old men came to meet them. They talked excitedly of the day's hunt, the absence of injury to the hunters and the success that meant full bellies for the coming winter months. Always, the specter of famine stalked the people; never was it far from the minds of men and women, survivors of other, leaner winters.

Once back in camp, the women sliced the meat into strips and hung it on the drying racks. The men saw to their weapons and tools, making them ready for the next day's hunt. Hezekiah was dismayed to find himself more inclined to watch White Water Woman than to tend to his own business. He had no desire to settle among the band, and would not acknowledge, even to himself, the wish to marry and raise a family. Still, White Water Woman drew his eyes and pulled his emotions to herself. When Killer of Bears invited him to share a meal and sleep in the tipi, it was beyond his power to refuse.

It began to sprinkle just about the time it got too dark to work outside. The women went in then, and set to work preparing supper. White Water Woman picked up an armload of wood from the stack near the tipi door and carried it inside. She built up the fire and while it was burning down into cooking coals, she prepared water lily bulbs for roasting and corn meal for mush. When the coals were right, she set some strips of buffalo meat on green sticks over the coals to roast. She wrapped the water lily bulbs in a nest of grass and cottonwood leaves and put

178

them among the coals. She boiled some water in a small cast iron kettle that Killer of Bears had traded beaver skins for and sprinkled corn meal in. She stirred it as it cooked so that it was smooth and free of lumps.

Killer of Bears was elderly, nearly sixty, but still strong and able to do his share of hunting and fighting. He wore his mostly white hair in long braids wrapped in fur and decorated with feathers and shell disks, except the front, which he wore in a tall brush. He sat at the back of the tipi, leaning against a beaded backrest, the only one in the tipi. Hezekiah sat on his right.

Hezekiah let his hair curl as it would and only bothered to comb it now and then, when he happened to think of it. Like Killer of Bears, he wore buckskins but he preferred boots to moccasins, tall black boots. Those boots fascinated White Water Woman but she disciplined herself not to look at them, just as she kept her eyes down and never looked rudely into the eyes of either man.

Killer of Bears and Hezekiah talked while she worked but she didn't concern herself with their conversation, it was only about the day's hunt and to her one hunt was much like another. She ladled mush into wooden bowls and served first her husband, then her guest. Spoons were fashioned from buffalo horn. White Water Woman sat to eat her mush, carefully folding her legs to one side of her body in the proper feminine posture. When she stood to serve the rest of the meal, she rose gracefully, all in one motion, as was fitting in a well-bred Absoroka woman.

After supper, Killer of Bears lit a soapstone pipe that had a horse head carved on the bowl, while Hezekiah smoked his plain wooden pipe from the States. The two men talked, telling tales of their travels, mostly. Killer of Bears knew of the Pacific Ocean, though he had never traveled as far as that, and was interested to hear Hezekiah's account of the Atlantic Ocean. Hezekiah had been to New Orleans once as a very young child and retained vivid impressions of the city and the Gulf of Mexico, but he had never seen an ocean.

Presently, White Water Woman rose and went outside for more wood. The raindrops sparkled in her hair as she stooped over the fire to bank it for the night. She moved clockwise around the tipi, spreading bearskins and buffalo robes to make two beds, one at the rear of the room, the other to one side.

Killer of Bears rose and emptied his pipe dottle into the fire. Hezekiah did likewise. The men stripped off their clothing and got into bed. White Water Woman got into bed beside her husband and wiggled out of her dress. She placed it on the floor near her head and tucked the bearskin robe over herself. Killer of Bears reached for her and pulled her close. Accommodatingly, she fitted her body to his, permitting his embrace, knowing it was not amorous but merely comfortable. She glanced at Hezekiah and, seeing that he was watching her, quickly averted her eyes.

The next morning was chilly but clear. The rain hadn't amounted to much more than enough to settle the dust. White Water Woman pegged out the buffalo hides that Killer of Bears had gotten the day before. She finished slicing the meat and hung it on the drying racks. All around her other women were doing similar work. That afternoon, when all the meat was on the racks, she went into her tipi and came out carrying her riding tack. As the day before, she caught Walks Like a Cougar and rode first out onto the prairie and then up into the hills. Once more she bathed in the pool at the foot of the waterfall. She prayed that she might remain strong and firm of purpose.

That evening she went into the menstrual lodge, which was set at the edge of the camp, where the inmates were separated from the daily life of the people. She lay on a bed of buffalo robes across the fire from another woman. Spotted

Lily Woman was eighteen, pretty, and well-groomed. She was eating a strip of broiled buffalo meat.

"I guess I'm really lucky," Spotted Lily Woman said, "I never have cramps."

"You are very lucky," affirmed White Water Woman. "It wouldn't be so bad if I could be at home, doing my regular work. At least that would take my mind off it, instead of being here with nothing to do but think about it."

"I think it's nice to have the rest."

"Well, yes, you have something to rest from. The children require a lot of time and attention."

Spotted Lily Woman smiled. "I was rather hoping that I would be pregnant again."

White Water Woman smiled at her. "Maybe next month."

"Maybe. Would you like to play the dice game?"

"Not tonight, Spotted Lily Woman. I'm going to try to sleep away this pain."

"Good night, then."

Spotted Lily Woman spread her robes to make a bed and White Water Woman turned her back to the fire and closed her eyes.

Inside her tipi, Killer of Bears and Hezekiah were sitting, talking and smoking. Hezekiah looked around, puzzled.

182

"White Water Woman is not in the tipi tonight?" he ventured.

"It is her time to stay in the menstrual lodge."

"Oh. Oh, I see."

"Your friend, the other white man, was not in camp today."

"He's gone back to the mountains. To the beaver streams."

Killer of Bears kept his face expressionless but inwardly he wondered why the two white men had not gone to the beaver streams together. They had been partners for several years and he knew of no reason for the partnership to end at that time. No reason but one: that Hezekiah could not tear himself away from the proximity of White Water Woman. It was a thought that saddened him.

The two men smoked in silence until their pipes were finished. Killer of Bears emptied his pipe into the fire and Hezekiah did likewise. Killer of Bears banked the fire for the night and they went to bed.

A week later the Indians broke camp. The men caught the horses and prepared most of the travois. The women packed their household goods and took down the tipis. White Water Woman was inside her tipi, packing her clothes in rawhide boxes. She picked up two full boxes and started outside with them but dropped one. The contents spilled out and she sighed with exasperation as she stooped to repack the box. Hezekiah entered, saw what had happened and began to pick things up. White Water Woman was scandalized.

"What are you doing?" she demanded. "You must not be here now."

"Why not?" Hezekiah asked, knowing quite well that he was violating the etiquette of the Absorokas.

"It will make a scandal."

"For you to be in here alone with this child in the middle of moving camp?"

"For you to be doing women's work," she corrected.

Hezekiah laughed. "Oh. Well, I just came to ask if you need any help."

White Water Woman replied scornfully, "To take the tipi down? No, of course not."

Hezekiah grinned at her and went out. He put his head back in. "No offense, ma'am."

She laughed and Hezekiah left to help out with the horses. White Water Woman went back to her packing. She took the boxes out and then took the tipi down. She used two of the poles to make a travois and folded the tipi covering. Spotted Lily Woman helped her load it on the travois. When everything was loaded onto the travois or stowed in rawhide panniers on the horses, behind the riders, the Absorokas mounted and rode out in single file.

The women and children rode the horses pulling the travois and carrying the panniers. The men were fully armed and rode as guards, keeping a careful watch for enemies. White Water Woman looked at Killer of Bears and her heart was full of love and pride at the picture he made, sitting his big, pinto stallion with all his weapons about him. She was glad to know that she had never touched his warrior's accoutrements, had never done anything that would diminish his power to make war or to curtail his skill in hunting. She knew she would always be safe when her husband was near.

They rode up into the mountains for several days, halting at last in a little valley. The aspens along the creek were golden, radiating their lovely, glowing light that was more than reflected sunshine. White Water Woman set up her tipi on a level space, carefully facing the door to the east. The evergreen forest on the mountainsides afforded a background of great beauty, as well as providing firewood, food, and shelter from the winds.

The huckleberries were ripe and the women and children took basketry containers and rode to one of the patches. This was one of the happiest times of the year and there was much laughter and chatter as they picked berries. The bears were also after the berries but, with all the noise they were making, they knew that the bears would seek other patches. White Water Woman filled several containers with the plump purple berries. Her fingers were stained with their juice as she affixed the lids and fastened the containers on Walks Like a Cougar. Spotted Lily Woman and one of her children were going after more baskets as they passed by.

"I'm going to bathe before I go home this afternoon," White Water Woman said.

"Watch out for bears," warned Spotted Lily Woman automatically. But she was preoccupied with her children and berry-picking and didn't really have any attention to spare for anyone else that afternoon.

White Water Woman smiled at her and mounted her mare. She rode up the trail, past the berry patch. As she rode through the pines, she saw columns of steam rising through the trees. She rode on until she came to the river. Where a tall plume of steam rose, fluffy white into the deep blue autumn sky, a hot spring flowed over the bank and into the river. Colonies of lichen made the riverbank a wonderful array of colors, reds and golds, greens and blues, all opalescent in

186

the bright sunlight. A moose with her calf stood in the river and watched horse and rider a minute before walking away upstream.

White Water Woman led her mare to a spot above the spring and knelt to drink. She dropped the reins and Walks Like a Cougar drank then wandered over to a grassy spot and began to munch. The woman stripped off her clothes and unbraided her hair. She waded into the river where the hot spring warmed it. The water was just deep enough, with a bottom of smooth pebbles, to make a perfect place to bathe. White Water Woman closed her eyes, luxuriating in the sensuous delights of sunlight and warm water and the beauty and serenity of the forest that surrounded her.

"I've been looking for you." Hezekiah stepped out into the clearing. He wore a white and blue Hudson's Bay blanket that had been made into a coat.

"I know."

He sat on a log near the pool. "Why don't you divorce your husband?"

"Perhaps I'm in love with him."

"No. You're not. I've seen how it is between you. And I know that it's different among the Absoroka than among the whites in the settlements. You aren't bound to him any longer than you want to be."

"Is that true? That white women must remain married no matter what their wishes?"

"Yes. Death is the only release for white women when their marriages are not satisfactory."

"Whose death? Hers or her husband's?"

"Either."

"Is it the same for black white women? The women of your people?"

"No. Most of my people are slaves. They are owned by white men and forced to do what the white men tell them to do. Sometimes they pretend to be married but it only lasts as long as the white men don't sell one or the other of them."

"Sell? Do you mean like rifles and furs?"

"Yes. Exactly like that."

White Water Woman flicked a glance at him and was startled to see the bitter pain in his face.

"I do not seem to be able to understand the ways of white men. Do they sell the black white men's babies and children, too?"

"Sometimes. Babies stay with their mothers but children are often sold to other white men."

"Turn your back so I can come out of the water."

Hezekiah stood and took his coat off, holding it out to her. "Here, you'd better put my coat on."

"I have my own clothes."

"Don't be stubborn. Your dress won't keep you warm like the coat will."

"I didn't know white men were so kind."

"I'm not a white man. I'm a black man."

"Yes, a black white man."

"No, just a black man."

"Yet you are like the white men."

"Not really. You only think that because white men are different from Absorokas and so are black men. You don't think Shoshones and Shawnees are just alike, do you?"

"No, there are many differences. Every tribe of people is different from all the others. Yet, they are alike, too."

"It's the same with black people and white people. And with whites and whites and blacks and blacks. Everybody is different."

White Water Woman's skin was beginning to pucker, she had been in the water so long. "Are you going to turn your back? Or not?"

"Will you come out if I don't?"

"No."

Hezekiah put the coat on the log and turned his back. He wanted very much to turn around but he managed to keep his back turned to her. As soon as she was reasonably sure that he would not peek at her, she waded to the bank and slipped his coat on. It was warm and soft and smelled of tobacco and Hezekiah.

"Can I turn around now?" he asked plaintively.

"Yes."

He turned to watch her bend over and squeeze the water out of her long black hair. She went to her horse and took a porcupine tail brush out of her saddlebag then sat on the log to detangle her hair. Hezekiah sat down near her and watched.

White Water Woman was a realist. Absoroka women had to be in order to survive. She found this black man indescribably exciting. She was conscious of his every move, every gesture, every breath. She was aware that his breathing had quickened, that he was restraining himself with difficulty. That awareness added to her own excitement. She made one last protest.

"I have no wish to divorce my husband. He is a good man, a good husband. It would grieve him terribly. I cannot do it."

Hezekiah spoke softly. "I love you, White Water Woman. I want you to be my wife."

"I cannot."

She put the brush down and rose to her feet. She stood in front of him, letting the coat fall open. He looked up into her face incredulously. Then a look of joyous anticipation spread across his features. She knelt in front of him and he pulled her close.

190

White Water Woman, dressed again, sat on the log, looking at the shimmering river bank where the spring water glided silently over the lichens and into the river. Hezekiah buckled his belt and sat beside her.

"What happens now?" he asked.

"Now I ride back to camp. In a little while, you ride back to camp."

"Killer of Bears is not a fool. He'll know right away."

"Yes, he will know."

"He'll beat you."

White Water Woman looked at him sadly. "He won't beat me. He needs me."

"He'll have me burned at the stake or something."

"White men have the strangest ideas about such things. Do white people execute each other for infidelity?"

"Well, not actually. Not officially. Not unless it's a queen or someone like that."

"All that will happen now is some gossip."

That evening Killer of Bears leaned against his backrest, watching White Water Woman prepare the meal. She stirred the kettle of stewed buffalo and ladled some into a wooden bowl. She took it to her husband and handed it to him with a horn spoon. She ladled a bowl of stew for herself and sat down. They ate in silence, White Water Woman tried to suppress her glow of happiness but without much success.

After the meal was finished, Killer of Bears smoked his pipe and White Water Woman got out a deerskin dress and began to sew on ornaments of shell and elks' teeth. It was at bedtime that White Water Woman discovered how much harder it would be to lie next to her husband than she had expected it to be. She lay beside him as usual but when he put his arm around her waist, she stiffened in silent protest, hating the hypocrisy she had decided to practice. She forced herself to relax and Killer of Bears pulled her against him. It was the last time he touched her.

Hezekiah waited for her each afternoon at the hot spring on the riverbank and she met him there every day. She felt like a girl again, reckless and silly, giddy with love. In her heart she knew it couldn't last but she could not bring herself to deliver the last blow to Killer of Bears. She would stay with him as long as she could. Hezekiah fretted and reproached her for hard-heartedness to him. Finally, late in the autumn, when the band was preparing to go into winter camp high in the mountains, he told her that he would seek out his trapping partner when they broke camp.

White Water Woman was dismayed. "I do not

want you to leave," she told him. "How can I bear to be without you? You are my entire happiness, my only joy."

"How can I bear to go on like this?" he countered. "Knowing that you are mine for an hour in the afternoon and his the rest of the time. It's driving me crazy to know that you sleep in his arms."

"Why? I told you he is incapable. Anyway, he no longer takes me in his arms."

He was impatient with her obtuseness. "I want you to sleep in my arms. I want you to be my wife. I want you to bear my children."

"I will promise this much – I will sleep apart from Killer of Bears and if I find I am to bear your child, then I will divorce him."

"I hate this sneaking around. I want to share your tipi. I want everyone to know how it is with us. How much I love you."

White Water Woman laughed. "Do you think everyone does not know where we are and what we are doing?"

"Damn it, I want respectability."

But Hezekiah knew that it was beyond his power to leave her and she knew it, too. She put her arms around him and laid her head against his chest. He crushed her to him and prayed for a son.

It was some weeks later, when they were in

winter camp high in the Absoroka Range of the Rocky Mountains, that White Water Woman brought an armload of firewood into the tipi and put it down near the door. Killer of Bears was sitting by the fire, affixing arrowheads to arrows.

"It's going to be quite a storm, I'm afraid," she said, stamping the snow off her moccasins. "The snow is already ankle deep."

"Good. It's a good time to raid a Blackfoot horse herd."

White Water Woman put some wood on the fire then sat down and took up her work. Using an awl, she punched holes in the edges of some rawhide squares then threaded them through with buck-skin thongs to form boxes. She had already painted the sides and top pieces with geometric designs in shades of brown and red.

"I wish you wouldn't go," she said. "We have all the horses we need."

"Perhaps it is not horses that I'm going for."

"What then? Everyone is aware that your coup stick is well-decorated with many valorous deeds."

"You have packed the pemmican?"

"Yes. But I wish you wouldn't go. These forays are for the youngsters. Let them win their honors."

"Have you also packed my extra moccasins?"

"Yes. And your fur leggings. But I tell you plainly that you are foolish for going. There is nothing to be gained."

Killer of Bears was well aware that there was nothing to be gained by going on a raid against their Blackfoot neighbors. Nothing except his pride. He had always been a respected warrior, his coup stick was hung with tokens of the many braveries he had undergone for the sake of his people and his place among them. It was the greatest disappointment of his life that he had been unable to beget sons and daughters to fill his heart with joy. He did not blame White Water Woman for going to the black white man for what he could not give her. He appreciated her kindness and loved her as he always had. But it was hard to know that the whole band knew of his humiliation and gossiped behind his back. He would go with the young men the next morning and try to regain some of his self-respect.

Before dawn the warriors mounted their horses. They were painted for war and carried their weapons and shields. Hezekiah was going along and was much excited at the prospect of stealing horses to sell to the traders at Bent's Fort. If he could steal three or four good horses, he could sell them for enough to supply himself for a couple of years in the mountains, even if he didn't do any trapping. White Water Woman was sure to become pregnant soon and he would take her away from these people and build her a snug cabin where they could be happy together. He knew exactly where to build it.

White Water Woman stood at the edge of the camp and watched Killer of Bears and Hezekiah mount their horses with the other warriors. The whole population was there to see them off. She turned abruptly, pulling her bearskin robe closely about her, and went back to her tipi. She was angry with the two men in her life, that they could be so gaily going off on a raid, knowing the dangers. It was completely unnecessary for either of them to go.

The Absoroka war party rode three days to reach a Blackfoot winter camp. Just before dawn on the fourth day they left their own horses with a small guard in a fir coppice and approached the Blackfoot horse herd on foot. They worked their way around so they would come upon the herd facing into the wind. The moon had set but the stars were bright in a cloudless sky. The Blackfoot camp was separated from the herd by the wide meadow and a creek. It gave the appearance of a populace deeply asleep. Even the dogs were quiet.

Hezekiah had looped lassos around the necks of two fine horses and was just about to lead them away when the Blackfoot camp suddenly erupted into furious activity. The Absoroka warriors, including Hezekiah, took to their heels, leading the horses they had their ropes on and making as much noise as they could to spook the others so they'd be hard to catch and so impede the pursuit. Even so, a number of Blackfoot warriors managed to catch mounts and race after the raiders in an astonishingly short time. The Absorokas had only time to reach their own mounts and get started before the Blackfoot warriors were after them.

The Absorokas were closely followed and presently pursued and pursuer broke out of the forest and down a long sagebrush slope to the river. There was a running fight along the river bottomland with a lot of shooting, both of bows and muskets. Marksmanship being what it is from the back of a running horse at the distance between the two war parties, no one was hit until Killer of Bears abruptly turned his horse and galloped toward the Blackfoot warriors. One of his companions saw what his intention was and tried to stop him but was too late. Killer of Bears caught the enemy by surprise and was able to shoot his bow and hit one and to touch two of them with his coup stick before falling. The Absorokas were forced to leave his body behind.

The people in the Absoroka camp were

gathered to welcome the war party back. Each warrior brought at least one horse and a couple of them led three. Hezekiah looked for White Water Woman, wondering what the death of Killer of Bears would mean for them. The people were gladdened at the sight of so many horses but became solemn when they saw that Killer of Bears had not returned. Hezekiah slowly approached White Water Woman, helpless in the face of convention to comfort her. The leader of the little war party handed the lead ropes of his prizes to one of his young sons who had come to greet the returning warriors. He walked up to White Water Woman.

"He's dead, isn't he?" White Water Woman asked, knowing the answer. "My husband is dead."

"Yes," the warrior answered. "Your husband is dead. He died valiantly."

White Water Woman began to wail in the customary mourning fashion for a fallen warrior. She turned quickly and walked to her tipi. Still wailing, she snatched up a knife and gashed her palm. Hezekiah entered the tipi. As she raised the knife to gash her cheeks, he saw her intent and, horrified, grabbed her wrist.

She struggled to free herself. "Let me go. I must sacrifice for my husband."

"You shall not disfigure yourself for a man you didn't love."

White Water Woman tried to take the knife in her left hand. "He was my husband!"

Hezekiah took the knife from her and she collapsed in his arms, sobbing. He tossed the knife away and held her tenderly, whispering endearments.

A scandalously short time later, White Water Woman and Hezekiah decided to leave the camp and move up into the mountains where he could trap beaver. He sold all but three of his horses, getting a musket, ammunition, and a number of beaver and otter pelts in exchange. He and White Water Woman loaded the tipi and all their goods on two travois. She would ride her appaloosa mare, who pulled one travois and lead the horse that pulled the other one. Hezekiah would ride his chestnut gelding and lead his other horse. When all was ready, Spotted Lily Woman came to bid her friend goodbye.

"You'll come to visit next summer?" she pleaded as they embraced.

"My husband has promised that I may visit with you while he goes to the rendezvous. It will be only one snow."

"I'll miss you, White Water Woman."

"I'll miss you, too. I'll miss everyone, but you

most of all."

White Water Woman mounted Walks Like a Cougar and followed her new husband out of the camp.

Hezekiah led the way through the pine woods, up higher into the mountains, following the river. Several days later they chose a sheltered spot on the river bank, near a hot spring, to make their home. White Water Woman pitched the tipi while Hezekiah took care of the stock and quickly put together a brush corral. By the time he came in that night, she had supper cooking in an iron kettle. Hezekiah seated himself on the right side of the fire, sitting cross-legged. The backrest, along with the rest of Killer of Bears personal property had been burned.

White Water Woman looked at Hezekiah with some dismay. "That is the place where guests sit." She pointed at the place opposite the door. "That is where my husband sits."

"I like it here," Hezekiah remarked.

"You prefer to be a guest?" she asked, puzzled. "You don't wish to be my husband after all?"

"I am your husband and I prefer to sit here."

"White people are very strange," White Water Woman remarked.

She filled a wooden bowl with venison stew

200

and took it to him with a pewter spoon. He ate with enjoyment and she filled a bowl for herself and sat across the fire from him.

"Tomorrow I'll teach you how to make biscuits," Hezekiah told her.

"Biscuits?"

"It's a sort of bread we make with flour."

"The white powder you bought at the fort?"

"Yes."

He finished his stew and put the bowl down. He found his pipe, filled and lighted it, and sat smoking contentedly. White Water Woman got out a pair of moccasins and worked on applying the porcupine quill bead decorations. When Hezekiah cleaned out his pipe, she put the moccasins away and spread buffalo robes at the back of the tipi to make a bed. Hezekiah put some wood on the fire, undressed, and got into bed. White Water Woman undressed then noticed that the door flap was not quite secure. She went to remedy that and then got into bed. He reached for her and she snuggled against him.

"Oh," he yelped, "you're cold."

"Warm me," she whispered.

Until the beaver ponds froze over, Hezekiah trapped industriously, standing in the bone-chilling water to pull the caught beavers out and reset the traps. He took them back to the tipi where he skinned them and fastened the pelts to round wooden frames. White Water Woman roasted the tails and stored the rest of the meat.

Occasionally, Hezekiah took his gun and went hunting so they had deer and elk venison, as well as the jerked buffalo and fresh beaver. White Water Woman brewed a kind of tea from pine needles and insisted that Hezekiah join her in drinking a cup of it every day. It would keep his teeth from falling out, she told him. He regarded that as a quaint Indian superstition but humored her in drinking the astringent tea. It didn't taste all that bad but it wasn't all that delicious, either.

Some of their most delightful hours were spent in the river. Where the hot spring drained into the river, the water was comfortably warm, even with snow on the ground. They would leave their clothes in the tipi and walk down to the river wrapped in buffalo robes.

One afternoon they were lying in the water, lazily enjoying the warmth of the water and the beauty of the snow-covered forest.

"White Water Woman," Hezekiah murmured.

"Mmmmm?"

"Nothing. I just wanted you to look at me like that."

"Like what?"

"Like you love me."

"I didn't know it would be like this. I didn't know I could be so happy."

"Neither did I," Hezekiah answered. He lifted her hand and kissed the palm. "I think this must be paradise."

"There will be another to share our paradise in the summer."

"You're going to have a baby?" He sat up straight and spoke excitedly.

She smiled at him. "Yes."

His face lighted up. "I'm going to be a father." He became thoughtful at once. "I wonder if I'll know how." He looked at his wife in sudden alarm. "Should you be here in the water? Is it too cold? Is it too hot?"

She laughed. "It is not too cold nor too hot. I am fine."

Hezekiah stood up. "I think we'd better go back inside. You need to rest."

White Water Woman protested but allowed him to pull her to the bank and wrap a robe around her. He pulled the other robe around himself and hustled her quickly up to the tipi where he insisted that she lie down while he bustled around, building up the fire and piling additional robes on her.

Her pregnancy was completely normal. As the

winter wore on, she grew rounded and happier. She busied herself with making a backrest for Hezekiah. She decorated it richly with shells and beads and he found himself oddly touched when she presented it to him and covered it with furs to make it soft. She was puzzled by his continued refusal to sit in the husband's place in the tipi but no amount of persuasion moved him.

He made them each a pair of rawhide snowshoes and after that they spent quite a lot of time walking in the woods. The beauty and peace permeated to their very souls, obliterating the remnants of guilt concerning the death of Killer of Bears. They looked forward serenely, with confidence. Sometimes it seemed to each of them that they had never known any life but this one together. Hezekiah's early years of struggle against a slave-owning majority race, the privations his mother suffered, her sorrow in not being able to shield her children from the indignities visited up them, all the bitterness of servitude receded from his consciousness. His joy was complete and in the profound rapture of the moment, he unthinkingly expected it to go on forever.

White Water Woman loved the snowshoe treks with Hezekiah but almost as much she loved the hours they spent inside the tipi, working together.

She made a cradleboard and decorated it with her choicest shells and beads. She ornamented it with white deerskin fringing and laced a soft deerskin cover over it. Hezekiah made parfleches of rawhide and White Water Woman painted them. He made fishhooks, awls, and other small utilitarian items out of bone, stone, horn, and wood. One morning she broke the wooden spoon she used when cooking in the iron pot. Hezekiah spent nearly the whole day in carving a new one; a grouse in full display adorned the inside of the bowl and incised vines climbed up the handle, twining round and round.

They decided to stay in the mountains except for one brief visit to the rendezvous. Hezekiah had traded his furs for powder and lead, flour, corn meal, seashells, and beads. He had also bought a quantity of abalone shell jewelry for White Water Woman. She was richly and elaborately dressed for the mountain men, like their Victorian brothers in the States, liked for their women to reflect their success and prosperity in their gowns and jewels.

White Water Woman visited with the wives of other mountain men and reflected on the oddness of white men. They were, it seemed to her, the silliest people God ever made. They spent a year in gathering many more beaver pelts than they could ever possibly use. The work was hard and miserable. Then they met at the rendezvous, sold their pelts for much money, and in a few days of profligacy spent it all on liquor and fancy jewelry and gee-gaws. They roistered and fought and drank and gambled. And when the rendezvous was over, many of them had to go into debt to the fur companies to outfit themselves for the next year. All in all, she was glad when it was time to return home.

During the spring and summer, Hezekiah hunted and chopped firewood and cut wild hay for the horses' winter fodder. White Water Woman dried the meat and cured the hides; she dug the bulbs and roots of various plants to dry for the winter; and she found time to sit in the sun and dream of her approaching motherhood.

One summer evening as they sat and watched the stars twinkle against the darkening twilight sky, Hezekiah broached the subject that he'd been secretly worrying about for some time.

"We best go to the camp of the Absorokas before the baby's born." He looked down at her to see how she took his words.

"I don't want to," she answered softly. Her labor pains had begun in the early afternoon but, not wanting to alarm her husband before it was necessary, she had concealed them from him. "I

206

want our baby to be born here, in our home."

"You can't expect me to deliver the child," he exclaimed. "I don't know anything about it."

"I have often assisted the midwife. I can tell you everything you need to do."

"There might something go wrong," the horrified Hezekiah told her, trying to keep the panic out of his voice. "You might die."

"I am not going to die in childbirth," White Water Woman said decisively. She put his hand on the mound that was the baby. "He's kicking. Feel him? He doesn't want to leave here either."

Hezekiah snatched his hand away as if her skin were burning hot. "All the same," he said adamantly, "we'll leave in the morning. You know it's best."

She smiled. "I'm not convinced but if you still want to go in the morning, we'll go."

He nodded, pleased with himself and with her reasonableness.

That night White Water Woman lay in bed, watching the little fire that was necessary at night at that high altitude even in summer. Hezekiah lay beside her, sleeping deeply. Toward morning, her contractions came with frequency and intensity. She moaned and Hezekiah woke, instantly alert.

"White Water Woman? What is it?"

"The baby."

"The baby's coming? Now?" Hezekiah was indignant. "It's too soon. You were supposed to go back to the camp for this." Then the full force of his predicament hit him. "Oh, my God. Wait a minute. Don't do anything rash. What am I supposed to do first?"

He jumped to his feet and pulled his clothes on.

White Water Woman laughed. "It's all right, Hezekiah. Be calm."

"Calm! Yes, all right. I'll be calm. Fire. We need to build up the fire."

He dashed outside and brought in a big armload of wood. He dumped it in an untidy pile and put some on the smoldering fire and stirred it up until it blazed. He looked around wildly, trying to think what he should do next.

"You might get some water and set it to heat," she suggested.

A contraction gripped her, causing her to clench her hands and her teeth. She moaned and Hezekiah knelt beside her, giving her his hand to squeeze. The pain eased and she smiled up at him.

"I think you'd better get the water now," she said.

"I can't leave you like this."

"Please?"

Hezekiah gave her an anguished look and

hurried to get the water. He brought in the iron kettle, filled to the brim with water from the hot spring. As he set the kettle on the fire, another contraction caused White Water Woman's body to twist. She cried out and he knelt at her side, giving her his hand once more.

"Are you all right?" he asked, his heart in his eyes, fearful for her safety, agonized that he couldn't stop her suffering.

She smiled through her pain. "Yes, of course." The pain passed and she relaxed her grip on his hand. "The water broke earlier – it won't be much longer now. I must get up."

She got to her knees and Hezekiah put a bear robe around her shoulders.

"What shall I do?" he whispered.

"Stand behind me and steady me. For now."

"For now? Oh, God."

Hezekiah suspected that something too trying for his masculine sensibilities was about to be thrust upon him but he had no alternative than to do as his wife directed him. White Water Woman's breath came fast and hard as she pushed her baby into the world.

"Hezekiah," she panted, "come and receive your child."

He followed her guidance and knelt in front of her. He gazed, awestricken, as their baby slipped into the world. He picked the baby up tenderly.

"It's a boy," he said softly.

"Of course it's a boy. You must hold him by the heels so he can breathe."

Hezekiah held the baby up and slapped his bottom. The baby bellowed indignantly while his parents smiled happily. In another time and place this soul would be known as Starla Mayhew.

White Water Woman sat in the sun outside the tipi, singing a lullaby to her son as he nursed at her breast. Hezekiah sat beside her, fashioning wooden hoops against the time he would need them for beaver pelts. He looked over at the picture his wife and son made, noting that the baby's skin was much lighter than his and had an underlying glow of bronze.

"He's beautiful, White Water Woman," he said. "Truly beautiful."

She smiled first at Hezekiah, then at the baby, who had fallen asleep. "What will you call him?"

"Shall it be an Absoroka name? Or a white man's name?"

"Are there no black names?"

"I only know one. It was my grandfather's."

"A pity. I would have liked him to have a black name."

Hezekiah was surprised and a little indignant.

"My grandfather's name is not acceptable? You haven't even heard it yet."

Now White Water Woman was surprised. "Does your grandfather still live, then, that you may speak his name?"

"No, but…Oh, I forgot. My people don't have a taboo against speaking the names of the dead. Would it make you uneasy to use my grandfather's name?"

"No, I don't believe it would. If it doesn't bother him, it shouldn't bother me."

"Micombero it is, then."

"Micombero. It's a pretty name. What does it mean?"

"I don't know."

"Micombero." She whispered the name to the sleeping baby.

On a balmy day in June the summer Micombero turned two, White Water Woman and Hezekiah sat in front of the tipi, which was pitched under some cottonwood trees. A small stream ran nearby. The wildflowers were in full bloom and a number of wild rose bushes bloomed pinkly among the trees. White Water Woman had been making a basket but it was on the ground, forgotten as she watched Micombero toddle around, exploring his world. Hezekiah was mending a headstall. He put his tools down and tested the strength of the mended strap by pulling it. Satisfied that it would hold, he attached the reins.

"Hezekiah," said White Water Woman, breaking a long, contented silence.

"Yes?"

"It's time to go back to my people."

"The rendezvous is next month."

"I don't mean for a visit. I mean to live."

Hezekiah dropped the headstall and stared at her. "I don't understand. I thought you were happy to live here with me and your son."

"I am. I can't imagine a greater happiness. But Micombero needs the tribe. He needs to learn the skills of a warrior."

"My teaching is not good enough?"

"Hezekiah, please don't be angry or offended." White Water Woman was distressed. She knew she had taken her husband by surprise but she knew no other way to tell him her determination, it was so clear to her that Micombero needed the Absoroka. "Your teaching is more than good enough for hunting and trapping. But a warrior needs the companionship of others his own age. He needs to grow up in the tribe so he'll have a home when you and I are dead."

"And what of me? Am I to be divorced or am I to become an Absoroka?"

"It is my prayer that you will come with us. You found life among us good once."

"When did you think to go?"

"Tomorrow."

Hezekiah gave her a long, bewildered look but she refused to meet his eyes. It was one of the things that continually rankled within him, her refusal to look him in the eyes. He never understood that the customs of her people forbade that intimacy between men and women. He picked up the headstall and went to the meadow where the horses were grazing. She watched as he caught his paint gelding and slipped the headstall over his ears. He mounted bareback and rode across the meadow, up into the forest.

Micombero grew to be a tall, handsome young warrior. He had great courage and was a fine horseman. In his early teens, his coup stick already told stories of daring deeds and reckless adventures.

After the first shock of White Water Woman's words that day under the cottonwoods, Hezekiah had realized that she was right. If Micombero was not to be adrift in the world, he would have to be accepted as a member of the Absoroka people. So Hezekiah made no further objections and the boy was brought up with the other boys to be a warrior. If Hezekiah sometimes regretted that only the color of his skin and a curliness to his hair that no amount of bear grease would straighten were the only evidence of himself in his son, he said nothing. Micombero was at least free, a proud man with a respected place among his people.

The youngster's vanity sometimes amused his father. He often thought of that other Micombero who'd been taken from his native land and brought to foreign shores to labor for the benefit of another man. That Micombero had been a proud and respected warrior, too. No doubt he'd been vain, as well. Somehow, Hezekiah felt, the circle was completed and the family had returned to its rightful place in the world.

White Water Woman took great pride in her handsome son. She spent a lot of her time and energy making his clothing with much embellishment of beads, feathers, fringing, and seashells. She had even traded for a number of copper cones that she sewed onto his leggings among the shells. It gave her great satisfaction to know that he was the most richly dressed young man in the entire region.

One day in late spring she came out of her tipi carrying a pair of highly ornamented moccasins. Micombero was standing a few feet from the door watching Dawn Woman, who was a pretty girl and had just become of marriageable age. Now she was sitting in front of her mother's tipi playing with a tiny cousin. The little one was toddling about, picking up pebbles and giving them to Dawn Woman. The girl gravely accepted them and held them in her cupped hands.

"Micombero," White Water Woman said.

"Yes, Mother?" He turned his attention to her.

She held out the moccasins. "I have finished your new moccasins."

"Thanks." He sat on the ground and exchanged the ones he was wearing for the new ones. "They're beautiful."

He stood up and White Water Woman watched him as he loped to the edge of the camp where the young men were gathering. Then she walked over to Dawn Woman and sat down beside her.

Micombero and several other young warriors stood while an elderly warrior, Fights the Wind, supervised their training exercise. It was one they had undertaken many times before. The camp was situated on the prairie where a little creek meandered through the buffalo grass. In the distance there was a slight rise in the land and a green patch marked where a small spring flowed. As Micombero waited for his turn, his friend, Shoots in Haste, complained.

"I hate this exercise."

"You always swallow the water," Micombero stated.

"Well, why not? I get very thirsty running all the way out there and back in this hot sun."

"Who doesn't?" replied Micombero. "But you'll never develop stamina by giving in to your body when you order it to do something difficult."

"I know."

Fights the Wind motioned Shoots in Haste forward. He exhorted the youngster to do better on this run, to speak to his body as he ran, to explain to his thirst that it would be assuaged when it was time, that until then thirst must be content to be ignored while the rest of his body did its work. Shoots in Haste filled his mouth with water and began the run to the spring and back.

Then it was Micombero's turn. Fights the Wind wasted no breath in telling Micombero what he already knew. The young man filled his mouth and began to run.

Fights the Wind stood and watched as the young warriors receded into the distance, becoming smaller and smaller until they were almost lost to sight. One by one they grew larger as they returned to camp, racing to return at least in the same order as they set out, not wanting to be outrun by any of their fellows. As they came

216

back to their starting point, they stopped in front of Fights the Wind. Those who could empty their mouths of the water they'd started with stood tall in his approbation, those whose mouths were empty had to endure his scorn. Micombero was one of the few who successfully completed the exercise and were allowed to drink. Dawn Woman watched from her place by her mother's tipi and rejoiced that Micombero was in the first rank. He would be a celebrated warrior one day.

Micombero and the others went next to archery practice. As White Water Woman sat in front of her tipi, sewing dentalium shells on a buckskin shirt, Hezekiah returned from exercising his horses. He brought his backrest and pipe from the tipi and settled down beside his wife. He sat smoking in silence for some time.

"It's time Micombero married," he said.

"I think he and Dawn Woman will marry. Unless you have someone else in mind?"

"No, let the boy marry where he loves."

"Ordinarily, I wouldn't agree with that but in this case, his fancy takes him where I think his best chance for a good wife lies. She is a thrifty cook, well-versed in the skills of gathering and preserving food. And she sews very well."

"She's a pretty little thing, too." Hezekiah remarked.

217

"As if that mattered," White Water Woman huffed.

"Of course it matters. Do you imagine a man doesn't care how his wife's face looks when they make love? Don't you care how I look when you look up at me in the firelight? I always thought it was my face that made your passion flame."

White Water Woman was embarrassed. "Not only your face," she murmured. Something akin to indignation was in her voice as she asked, "Is it only my face, then, that you care for? Not my being? Because, if so, you must have lost your love for me long since."

"Do I behave as if I no longer love you?"

"No. No, you don't." She smiled reminiscently. 'But I am no longer beautiful. My face is lined and my hair is streaked with gray and my body is not firm and rounded as it was."

"You are still beautiful. When I look into your face, I see the beauty of your love for me. I see myself – my best self – reflected in your caring. And it makes a man of me."

White Water Woman was deeply moved. "Oh, Hezekiah. These are things I haven't thought of before. Beauty is important, then, but not the beauty of the body – the beauty of the spirit."

Hezekiah grinned at her. "Well, it all seems to be mixed up together somehow."

He stood and held out his hand to her. She took it and rose.

"Where are we going?" she asked.

"Inside, to test these conclusions."

She smiled mischievously and went into the tipi; Hezekiah followed her.

Micombero and Dawn Woman were alone in a grove of cottonwoods. The sky was overcast and a few drops of rain fell. Dawn Woman stood with downcast eyes, leaning against a tree trunk. Micombero stood very closely in front of her. He tipped her chin up and kissed her.

The sky darkened and in the distance lightning cracked across the clouds; a few seconds later the thunder reverberated over the prairie. The rain began to fall with increasing volume. Micombero took Dawn Woman by the hand and ran with her into the shelter of an outcropping of rock that was almost a cave. They sat together, holding hands, watching the storm as it rolled closer. Micombero kissed her again, his passion echoing the passion of the elements. Dawn Woman's heart beat so that she could scarcely tell if it was her pulse or the thunder that she felt in her ears. Micombero knew he had found his wife.

One evening in the late fall, as White Water Woman, Hezekiah, and Micombero sat around their fire in the tipi, eating broiled buffalo steak and biscuits with honey, Micombero brought up a subject that he'd been consumed with for weeks. At last he saw his way clearly.

"Speaker of Truth is going to lead a raid against the Blackfoot. I shall go with him."

"You have added the new designs to your shield? The ones you saw in your dream?"

"Yes, Mother. I know I will be successful. I'm going to bring back enough horses to marry Dawn Woman."

White Water Woman and Hezekiah were very pleased.

"I hope you have no objections," Micombero continued, "because it's quite impossible to change my mind."

Hezekiah smiled upon his son. "Your mother and I have no objections. She is a nice, quiet, obedient girl. She will be a good wife for you."

"And she is beautiful," his mother added.

Micombero was puzzled at his mother's words because his people prized industry and skillfulness far above beauty and physical charms. However, Dawn Woman's beauty had by no means escaped his notice. "Yes," he agreed, "she is very beautiful."

Micombero had been on other raids against neighboring tribes but to raid the Blackfoot was every Absoroka warrior's especial joy. Armed and painted for war, the men followed Speaker of Truth to the edge of the meadow where the Blackfoot horses were pastured. False dawn was just beginning to lighten the eastern sky as the raiders crawled slowly and carefully toward the horses. Micombero had heard that some of the Blackfoot warriors tied long buckskin ropes around their favorite horse's necks and slept with the other end of the rope around their wrists. It was his plan to steal into the Blackfoot camp and take such a horse. Then he would ride bareback out into the meadow and drive off as many other horses as he could.

He moved silently into the camp and had just located a horse standing outside a tipi when the dogs began to bark. At first just one announced the presence of a stranger in camp but almost immediately all the dogs raised their voices in warning. Micombero deftly fastened the headstall that he carried onto the horse and dashed into the tipi with his knife drawn. The fire inside had burned to embers and the warrior and his wife were just waking when Micombero entered. The warrior sprang to his feet and the children awoke and began to cry. Micombero slashed the buckskin rope and, holding the end in one hand, touched his coup stick to the warrior with the other. He was gone so quickly that the Blackfoot could almost have believed he dreamed it.

Outside, Micombero mounted and galloped through the camp into the meadow. The Blackfoot followed but, seeing that he couldn't catch Micombero afoot and weaponless, returned to the tipi to prepare for pursuit. Micombero dashed in amongst the other raiders, who were also mounted bareback and who had also slipped headstalls over their prizes before mounting. They all whooped and yelled and made as much noise as possible driving the horses away from the Blackfoot camp, across the meadow to where they'd left their own horses tethered in the forest. All the way home Micombero exulted in the success of his enterprise and dreamed of his wedding with Dawn Woman.

A few days later, Micombero groomed the four horses that he had taken from the Blackfoot camp. He would like to have kept the one he took from the warrior who slept with his horse tethered to his wrist but he already had two fine horses and he wanted Dawn Woman to be his wife much more than he wanted anything else, even another fine war horse. On the morning of his wedding, Micombero dressed himself in his finest clothes, the little copper cones gleaming in the sun, and dressed his hair carefully with the pompadour standing high. He deplored the curliness of his hair but had long since given up trying to train it to lie straight. He put on all his jewelry.

Hezekiah and White Water Woman stood in front of the tipi and watched as their handsome son led four splendid horses down the avenue of tipis. He stopped in front of one and Dawn Woman's father stepped out. He examined the horses minutely then nodded to another warrior who took the lead shanks from Micombero and led them away.

Micombero followed Dawn Woman's father inside. A few minutes later, Micombero and Dawn Woman emerged from the tipi. White Water Woman, Hezekiah, and the bride's parents led the whole population of the camp in procession with the newly-weds to the tipi that Dawn Woman had prepared.

The rest of the day was given to feasting and gambling and horse racing to celebrate. Micombero was conspicuous for his bold and daring riding. Dawn Woman stood and watched, her pride and love in her eyes as her husband displayed his horsemanship. At nightfall, the drumming began and everyone joined in the dancing.

It was almost two years later that Dawn Woman went into labor with the first of their children. On a soft spring evening, with the stars winking brightly at a crescent moon, Hezekiah and Micombero sat outside Dawn Woman's tipi. From time to time there was a gasping cry from within, making Micombero extremely nervous. Hezekiah smoked placidly.

"How long does it take?" Micombero demanded, as Dawn Woman cried out again.

"I don't know. You birth is the only one I ever attended. I had no thought to spare for the time."

"I don't know how you did it. I'd rather fight a dozen Sioux and sixteen Blackfoot than listen to my wife's pain."

"Of course. You know how to fight your enemies. You don't know how to help your wife."

"I'm frightened, Father," Micombero confided. "What will I do if I lose her?"

"We all feel like that when our children are born. You won't lose her. She is a strong, healthy woman and the midwife is here and your mother. And her mother."

There was silence from the tipi and Micombero felt that the sudden quiet was the hardest of all to bear. Then, just as he was about to break his mother's commandment to stay outside, the baby began to wail. He relaxed somewhat and was heartened to hear the women murmuring. A few minutes later, White Water

Woman emerged, carrying the baby. She bent down and placed the baby in her son's arms, smiling at him. Hezekiah smiled at them both.

"You have a son, Micombero," she said.

Micombero looked up from the baby. "Dawn Woman?"

"Your wife is fine. In a few minutes you may see her."

Micombero put his finger in the baby's hand and grinned as the baby gripped it tightly. Dawn Woman's mother and the midwife came out of the tipi. Micombero rose and took the baby inside.

Dawn Woman was lying in bed. She smiled at Micombero and he smiled back, connected now with more than the love between husband and wife. The birth of the baby connected them to all those who had come before them and all who would come after them. They were transformed from being a couple to being a family. Now they were one of the foundation units of the tribe. They assumed the responsibilities of their parents for the safety and well-being of their people and their way of life. Something of this they sensed as they looked at their son and at each other.

A couple of days later the band moved camp. They rode in single file across the prairie. Coming to a river swollen with the spring run-off from the mountains, they crossed it as they had many times before. Most of the people were on the far side when White Water Woman rode her horse into the water. As the mare stepped, a rock caused a hoof to miss its footing and she fell. White Water Woman was swept from the saddle. She tried to grasp the horse's mane but the current was too swift. She was caught in the swirling, roiling water and pulled under. Hezekiah, who was riding with the rear guard, urged his horse into the river and leaped from the saddle to swim frantically toward the place where he last saw her.

Micombero, on the farther bank, heard the shouts of those who saw what was happening and turned to look. He was just in time to see his father leap into the water. He saw his mother's vacant saddle as her horse struggled out of the current downstream. Micombero knew the river well and he knew where the most likely spot for his parents to come ashore would be. It was a wide bend where the river slackened speed and made a shallow bottom for more than half its width, beyond the deep and swiftly flowing channel. Always there was a great pile of driftwood in that curve of the river.

As Micombero galloped around the bend, his father was pulling his mother's body out of the water onto the bank. She looked very peaceful. Micombero ran to them, thinking she looked almost as if she merely slept. But when Hezekiah fell to his knees and gathered her into his arms, Micombero saw that the limpness of death was upon her. Hezekiah looked up at him with the agony of shock and fearful loss in his face.

"I couldn't save her," Hezekiah said.

PART V

With a Spirit Soaring

Pat was lying back in the recliner with Dr. Parker sitting beside him, taking notes. He was in a trance, frowning, very troubled.

"I have to go home," he said. "I'm needed there. I've been putting off going back; I don't want to."

"What year is it, Richard?"

"1942."

"What is your job? Is it an important one?"

"A lot of people don't think so. I do, though. I'm a singer. And I think it's important to bring people a bit of entertainment, a little humor and respite from their troubles."

"Tell me what you're doing now."

Pat brightened, smiling dreamily. "I'm falling in love."

A good-sized crowd was dancing to the music of a band in a ballroom in Victoria, British Columbia. The American vocalist, Richard Kawashima, was of half Japanese ancestry. He was dressed in the most extreme current fashion that good taste allowed although his only jewelry was a heavy, carved gold ring. As he sang, his eyes kept returning to a special young woman.

Sheila Prior, destined to be Starla Mayhew in another life, was cutting a very fancy rug with a young man who danced as well as she did. She was dressed in a short skirt with a ruffled blouse. A golden St. Christopher medal hung around her neck. As they jitterbugged, her partner tossed her in the air, slid her between his legs, and spun her like a top.

At the end of the song, Richard and the bandleader took their bows and the band began to play an instrumental number. Richard hopped lightly off the bandstand and went to cut in on Sheila's partner. She smiled at him and his heart thumped in an unaccustomed manner. He had been just a little spoiled by the attention the girls lavished on him and was not used to being on the sending end of adulation.

After they had danced to a couple of songs, Richard maneuvered to an open french door and he and Sheila danced out to the terrace. It was delightful to hold her in his arms but he felt an imperative need to learn her name and a few other essential details about her. Never had he felt more intensely the need to know a woman. He asked her name and was glad to hear good old United States in her voice when she answered.

"Sheila Prior. What's yours?"

"Richard Kawashima. What are you doing here?"

"Dancing," she answered, looking at him as if she found him slightly mentally deficient.

"I mean, in Canada, not in this ballroom."

They strolled to the far end of the terrace and sat on the stone balustrade.

"I have a role in a ballet that's in rehearsal. We open a week from tonight."

"I'd never have guessed you for a ballerina. Not the way you jitterbug."

Sheila laughed. "Oh, well, it's all dancing. Where are you from?"

"The accent is confusing, isn't it? I was born in San Francisco. But I lived in London from the time I was eight until I was fifteen. And I've done a lot of traveling since then. So my accent's a little strange sometimes, even though I don't speak Japanese. That'd really put the cap on it, a Japanese accent mixed with the London and San Francisco ones."

"London. I'd like to go to London someday. I'd love to see a performance at Saddler's Wells."

"I saw one once. I'm afraid I wasn't very sympathetic, though. One isn't much interested in the ballet when one's a thirteen-year-old boy who's just made the cricket eleven. I don't even remember what they danced."

"It's ironic, isn't it? I'd almost sell my soul for a chance like that."

"May I watch you rehearse sometime?"

"If you're really interested. We're at the Bennington Theatre."

"Do you rehearse on weekends?"

"Not until Monday. Come around ten, while we're still fresh. We can get pretty bitchy later in the day."

"Why don't you come out with me tomorrow? I'll show you the Butchart Gardens."

Sheila looked at him speculatively.

"You'll like the gardens," Richard said. "Shall I pick you up at your place or meet you somewhere?"

"I'll meet you."

"In front of the Empress Hotel. Ten o'clock, we'll have breakfast."

"All right."

Richard slipped down from the balustrade and held out his hand to her. She took it and, before she could slip to the floor, he encircled her waist with his other arm and lifted her down. Holding her close, he danced her back into the ballroom. Her original partner, who was obviously looking for her, spotted them and hurried over. She smiled at Richard over the man's shoulder. Richard smiled back and went to the bandstand.

The next morning, after a grand breakfast at the hotel, Richard and Sheila took a cab out into the country. He wore slacks and a sport jacket with a white shirt and a green and purple tie. She wore a dress of navy blue, dotted with tiny white circles, and with a peplum. Her hat was small and white and lacy and her navy blue spectator pumps had spike heels. Sartorially splendid, they were a lovely couple.

As the cab drove along the two-lane blacktop, Richard asked where Sheila had been born.

She smiled with a touch of homesickness as the picture of her hometown flashed before her mind's eye. "Oregon. A tiny little town in the eastern part of the state called Mitchell. No one of any importance was ever born there or died there or anything. Since I left it, I've not met anyone who's ever heard of it."

"You're its only claim to fame?"

"Someday I will be."

"Are you the prima ballerina of your troupe?"

"Not yet," she answered seriously. "I have a lot more to learn. But I'm good."

"I'll reserve my opinion until I see you dance tomorrow. Which ballet are you rehearsing?"

"Cinderella. I'm one of the ugly step-sisters."

"That's casting against type with a vengeance."

The cab pulled up at the foot of a wide path. Richard stepped out and held the door for Sheila. He paid the fare and they walked up the path. Just inside the gate was a lath house hung with scores of baskets of begonias and fuchsias, all in full bloom. Inside, Sheila looked around at the blaze of color and reached out to gently touch a pink and purple fuchsia blossom.

"Begonias are okay, I guess," she said, "but I like fuchsias a lot better."

Richard nodded. "Fuchsias are so exotic. So lush and fragile-looking."

"And the most gorgeous colors." Sheila thought she had never seen anything as perfectly beautiful as the flowers in the lath house. "I'm so glad you thought of bringing me here, Richard."

"So am I."

They smiled at one another and left the lath house. They sauntered up the path, loving the beauty and serenity of the flowers and trees. There were a few other people on the paths, just as entranced with the loveliness as Richard and Sheila. The walls of an old quarry were covered with flowers and the path wound through the changing picture of delightful colors and forms. In a secluded corner, under a weeping cherry tree, Richard took her in his arms and kissed her. To his immense surprise, Sheila dealt him a stinging slap on the cheek. He let her go and stepped back.

"Did you mean that or was it just a move in the game?" he asked.

"You don't know me well enough to kiss me."

"Yes, I do."

"We only met last night."

'We've always known each other," he told her calmly.

He took her hand and she allowed him to draw her with him as he went on down the path, although she shot him several puzzled glances.

"I'd like to know how you figure that," she demanded at last.

"I don't know how. But last night when I looked out on the dance floor and saw you, I felt I'd found you after a long separation. You felt it, too."

"I felt something. I'm not sure what." Sheila looked at him quizzically.

"All right, I'll try not to rush you."

They rounded a low hedge and were in the rose garden. There were roses of all kinds, climbing roses, standard roses, tree roses, rambling roses, miniature roses, tea roses, damask roses, cabbage roses. Every shade of red, pink, white, and yellow gleamed in the sun. A tiny gazebo of wrought iron lace was covered with thousands of the yellow blossoms of *Lady*

Hillingdon. The scent of roses was almost dizzying. Or maybe it was their nearness to each other that seemed to set the world spinning askew on its axis. They loitered through the roses, stopping here and there to look at an especially lovely blossom. Forever after the sight or scent of roses would call up memories of that walk.

Sheila stood in front of the gazebo gazing at *Lady Hillingdon's* blooms and buds cascading down the black iron lace. She breathed deeply, drawing the heady scent into her very soul. Richard looked at her and a little frown puckered his forehead.

"Roses remind me of my mother," he said.

Sheila turned to him. "Thorny?"

Richard laughed. "No. Oh, no, mother's not thorny. Although she can be crabby. No, I meant that she's velvety like a rose petal."

He stepped over to some bushes of *Lady Sylvia*; Sheila went to stand beside him.

'See," he said, pointing to the deep pink heart of a perfect blossom, "velvety and sweet and feminine."

"That's a very nice picture of your mother. What's your father like?"

"He's more like a snapdragon. Handsome to look at but not as sociable as roses – keeping something of himself inside so that only a select

236

few ever get to know his innermost self."

"Snapdragon? Is he so formidable, then?"

"I don't seem to be doing so well at describing him as I did Mother. I don't know, maybe strangers do find him formidable. He's a gentle man, soft-spoken. He is – he was – a fabric designer. Right now he's very confused."

"What do you mean, fabric designer? Is he some kind of engineer?"

Richard blinked at her. "He designs cloth. The weave and colors and patterns. He was excited about rayon and nylon. He thought they could be very useful in making fine clothing available to people of modest means."

"What a fascinating job." Sheila wandered down a grass walk between a quarry wall covered with a tapestry of climbing roses and a row of tree roses with an edging of miniatures.

"It really is. The combinations of colors and weaving patterns are infinite. One of the things he misses most about living in the U.S. instead of Japan is that he's limited to wearing such drab clothing. He would love to wear the brocades and silks of men's robes in Japan.

"You said your father 'was' a fabric designer. What is he now? Why would he give up a job like that?"

"His parents immigrated from Japan. My

237

father is the Japanese-American half of my parentage."

"Oh." Sheila took a moment to process the information. "Oh, relocation. Oh, Richard, is your family in a relocation camp?"

"Not yet. They've been notified, of course. Mom said in her last letter that she thought they had about ten days to settle things up before they had to go. They're being sent to a place in northern California. Tule Lake."

"But why? Why do they have to go if they're American citizens?"

"Yeah." Richard tried to keep the bitterness out of his face and voice. "Due process and habeas corpus and all that. Do you want to know the real reason or the newspapers' version?"

"Well, I do occasionally read the newspapers – saboteurs and all that."

"Yes, there's a lot of loose talk. But, if you've noticed, there hasn't been even one actual case of sabotage brought against a Japanese-American. We're supposed to be sneaky and fanatically devoted to the Emperor. I'd like to see anyone more fanatically devoted than just about any good Democrat to Franklin Delano Roosevelt. Anyway, Pearl Harbor furnished the perfect excuse for locking up all the untrustworthy Japs. I'm surprised it's taken this long to get the program under way."

Richard reached for her hand and she allowed him to hold it as they strolled.

"You were going to tell me the real reason," Sheila prompted.

"Money. There are only about a hundred and ten thousand of us. That makes it safe to raid us for our property and businesses."

They were hardly aware when they left the rose garden and entered the Japanese garden. The formality of the clipped shrubs and the studied informality of the winding brook were a delightful contrast to the riot of color the roses made. A little red hump-backed bridge over the brook was shaded by a young flowering dogwood tree. They stopped at the apex of the bridge and leaned on the rail, looking down through the clear water to its pebbled bed.

Sheila glanced at him. "But can't you fight it in the courts?"

Richard shrugged. "We won't. Some might. My father feels that the only way to prove we are good Americans is to obey the president's order."

'But *you* don't have to go. You can't be forced to return to the States from Canada, can you?"

"That's not the point. I must go to help my family. Dad's not young anymore and Mom'll have her hands full with my sister and brother.

They need me. I've already waited longer than I should have. When they're settled, I'll enlist. If any branch of the service will have me."

"Enlist!" Sheila was indignant. "Maybe you should all be locked up. Why would you leave your family behind barbed wire and go and fight for the people who put them there?"

Richard smiled into her eyes. "It's my country, too."

Sheila slowly nodded her understanding.

"Now tell me about your family," Richard said.

"My dad's a rancher. Mom's a housewife, except she spends most of her time helping Dad with the ranch work."

"Are we talking cattle ranching here?"

"Yup. I'm an old cowhand."

"You ride and rope and move them little doggies along?"

Sheila laughed. "I used to. I miss my horse sometimes but I don't really miss the rest of it."

"So when did you have a chance to study ballet?"

Sheila grinned. "Weird, isn't it? I saw a picture of a ballerina in a magazine one day and just decided I wanted to dance like that. I must have made quite a fuss about it for a long time because Mom finally found a teacher. A lady who'd been a war bride in 1918. Mrs. Jackson. She's French. I've often wondered if she'd have married Mr. Jackson if she'd known where he lived."

"It must have been quite a shock for the poor lady to land in a little Oregon town from France."

"I imagine so. They don't even live in town; their place is about five miles up the canyon from Mitchell."

"Do you have brothers and sisters?"

"I have two brothers. They're seventeen and nineteen. Bud – he's the older one – wants to join the Navy but so far Dad's talked him out of it on grounds that someone's got to stay home and raise beef for the boys in uniform. Bobby has one more year of high school before he can enlist. I don't know him very well because I haven't been home much since he's been old enough to talk with."

Sheila gave Richard a rueful smile and left the bridge. He caught her hand again and they strolled into the Italian garden.

"Where did you study after you left Mitchell?"

"San Francisco. But I'd love to study at Saddler's Wells. Maybe after the war I'll get a chance. If I'm not too old by then. What's your dream?"

Richard was very definite. "After the war I'm going to find myself a beautiful girl, marry her, move to Hollywood and make movies and babies."

"Babies!"

"At least a dozen."

Sheila laughed. "She'll have to be a pretty special girl. Catholic, probably."

Richard maneuvered her into a pergola festooned with a profusion of pale lavender wisteria panicles. They sat down.

"She'll have to be a *very* special girl," Richard agreed. He took her in his arms and whispered, "Do I know you well enough yet?"

Sheila leaned back in his arms, looked deeply into his eyes, and kissed him.

That night and for nearly two weeks of nights, Sheila would stand near the bandstand at the ballroom, watching Richard as he sang. When he wasn't singing, he would jump down and they would dance. During the afternoons, he would sit in the theater, watching Sheila rehearse her role in *Cinderella*.

The afternoon of the dress rehearsal, Richard wasn't there. Sheila watched for him, growing more and more uneasy. Finally, as she danced with her "sister," taunting Cinderella that she couldn't go to the Prince's ball with them, she saw Richard walk down the aisle. He sat down and Sheila danced on. The wardrobe mistress approached the director and pointed at

Cinderella's raggedy dress. To Sheila's relief, the director called a break. The wardrobe mistress began to fuss with Cinderella's skirt. Sheila went down the steps to Richard. He rose to greet her and they kissed.

Sheila grinned at him. "What do you think? Is it funny?"

"Yeah," he answered, in a tone of some surprise. "It is funny. I didn't realize that you're a comedienne."

"Oh, you have no idea of the full extent of my talents. I have great range."

As they talked, Sheila led the way out to the lobby. It was deserted at that time of day so they had an unobstructed view of the enormous mural of the Canadian Rockies.

"I'm counting on that," Richard said.

Sheila studied his face. "You're leaving, aren't you?"

Richard pulled her close and she put her arms around him, dreading his answer.

"My bags are already at the station."

"It's no good asking you to stay." Sheila knew it was true but she hoped it was not.

"I'd give anything to stay," he said.

"Anything but your sense of duty."

"If I gave that, you wouldn't want me to stay."

She knew he was right. One of the things she

loved about him was his integrity. Although she appreciated it, she knew it was going to exact a price from her.

"What are we going to do?" she asked.

"Thank you for that, Sheila."

"For what?"

"For the acknowledgement that there is a 'we'."

"You have always been so sure of that."

"Yes, but not sure that you felt the same."

Sheila loosened her hold on him and stepped back to look at him. "I'll wait."

Richard led her to a sofa and they sat down, holding hands.

"I can't ask you to wait," he said earnestly. "I don't know if or when I'll be free again."

"Your family has been interned?"

Richard nodded. "I had a letter from Mom this morning. They've had to go to a center of some kind and they'll leave for Tule Lake day after tomorrow. If I leave this afternoon, I think I'll get there the same day they do. It's going to be hell for them but I may be able to help a little."

"You could enlist without going to the concentration camp first."

"Shhhh." Richard put his finger lightly on her lips. "Don't call it a concentration camp. America doesn't have concentration camps. We have relocation centers. For our own good, if you saw the Seattle paper today."

Sheila shook her head. "We could get married and I could stay with your family until you come home."

"No." Richard was vehement. "No. I can just bear to have my family imprisoned for the crime of having a different cast of feature and color of skin – and my mother isn't even guilty of that. I couldn't bear to have you caged in barbed wire, too. You stay free. Dance and do your job. If God is willing, we'll be together after the war."

"And we'll have that dozen children. Did you know that I'm a Catholic girl?"

Richard smiled at her. He lifted the St. Christopher medal from her chest. "I thought so. A good Catholic girl."

"Are you asking me if I'm a virgin?"

"No, I have no right to ask you that."

"Of course you have. And the answer is yes."

She took the medal from around her neck and put it around his. "St. Christopher will keep you safe for me."

Richard took off the carved gold ring he wore and put it on her left ring finger. "I love you, Sheila."

"I love you," she responded.

There were worlds of love and longing in their

eyes as they kissed. Gently, Richard broke the embrace and stood up. Sheila stood, too, and laid her head on his shoulder.

Richard whispered into her hair, "Go back to your rehearsal now. I mustn't miss my train."

Sheila nodded and lifted her head. They kissed again, long and passionately. Richard stepped away and, without looking back, went to the glass door and on through. Sheila watched him through the glass until he turned the corner. There were tears in her eyes as she went back into the theater to finish the dress rehearsal.

There was no passenger train to the Tule Lake Relocation Center but there was a station for the freight trains that stopped at the town of Tulelake, just north of the center. Richard left the train at Klamath Falls, the nearest passenger train depot, and managed to talk his way into the caboose of a Southern Pacific freight. When the train stopped at the tiny bustling town of Tulelake, Richard hopped off and stood surveying the scene. The depot was painted bright Southern Pacific yellow. The town was doing a brisk business and traffic jounced over the railroad tracks to Highway 139 in a two-way stream. The terrain was flat, surrounded by low hills on every side. The countryside was green with various crops.

Richard had not expected a cab rank, of course, but he had thought there might be a public telephone. He went into the office without bothering to remove his dark glasses. Three women and one man were at work at desks behind the counter. He set his suitcase down near the door and approached. One of the women left her desk to see what was wanted.

"Can I help you?" she asked with a smile.

"I'm looking for the Tule Lake Relocation Center."

"Oh, the Jap Camp. Sure. It's nine miles down the highway." She pointed to the south. "You can't miss it, it's the only thing there."

"Is there a taxi or car for hire in town?"

"The Chevy dealer might help you out. Or Jerry sometimes hires out as a cab. He's our freight man. Just a minute, I'll see if he's got time."

The clerk went into a back room, but failed to close the door. Richard could hear the entire conversation.

"Hey, Jerry. There's a guy out here wants a ride to the Jap Camp. You want to take him?"

"He a Jap? 'Cause I ain't takin' no goddam Nips for no ride."

"No, he's some kind of Limey, I think. The way he talks, anyway."

"He got any money? I ain't a charitable institution you know."

"No one would ever accuse you of being charitable. He looks prosperous enough. Come on, Jerry, yes or no?"

"Oh, all right. I could use a few extra bucks right now."

Jerry followed the clerk over to the counter. She smiled at Richard.

"Jerry says he'd be glad to drive you out," she said.

"Five bucks, mister. In advance," Jerry said.

Richard smiled at the clerk. "Thank you, ma'am."

He handed Jerry a five-dollar bill and pointed to his suitcase. "Bring my bag, boy."

Jerry shot him a look but pocketed the money and picked up the suitcase.

Jerry's car was a green DeSoto, not new. The drive to the relocation center only took a few minutes. Richard looked out at the crops. He recognized alfalfa and there were fields of grain but he didn't know what kind. And there was some kind of row crop that he would find out later was potatoes. As the DeSoto moved south, Richard saw an enormous rock bluff jutting out into the farmland, like a peninsula into a lake. At the foot of the peninsula and across the highway from it, was the Tule Lake Relocation Center. It was a desolate, ugly camp of tarpaper shacks arranged in rows along dirt streets. A high wire fence, topped with barbed wire, surrounded the camp and soldiers guarded the entrance gate.

Jerry stopped the DeSoto at the gate where armed guards stood ready to check people in and out. Jerry unloaded the suitcase and Richard removed his dark glasses and pulled his upper lip back from his teeth in imitation of the caricatures of Japanese soldiers that had sprung up everywhere. He unloosed a stream of sing-song gibberish that Jerry took to be Japanese. Outraged, he flung himself behind the wheel of the DeSoto and ground his gears in his haste to leave. Richard laughed and then turned to deal with the soldiers.

The guards gave him a bad time because of his lack of internment papers but he finally convinced them that he had a right to be confined behind barbed wire. He stopped at the administrative office and asked where his family was domiciled. He had known that the camp would be bare but he hadn't realized just how stark it would be. Knowing that once he'd talked his way in, he would not be allowed to leave without permission gave him a sick feeling of betrayal. Everything he'd ever known about his native land seemed to have become perverted and ugly. Let freedom ring? This was certainly a travesty of the hard-won freedom that so many thousands had died to establish and perpetuate.

He lugged his suitcase down the street, ankle deep in dust, until he reached the tarpaper shack that his family had been assigned to. Actually, it was half a shack, another family lived in the other half. He knocked on the door and his mother answered it. For a few moments they merely stared at one another. Then she flew down the steps to him and he dropped his suitcase to catch her in his arms.

"Richard." She clung to him as to a rock in a raging river. "Richard. Thank God you've come."

"Of course I came." Richard was shocked at his mother's emotion. She had always been of a cool disposition, rather priding herself on keeping calm under any circumstance. Now she was shaking and tears coursed down her cheeks. "You must have known I would come, Mom. I couldn't leave you to face this nightmare while I stayed safe in Canada."

"Oh, Richard." His mother could only hold tightly to him.

His father, his younger sister Megan, and his kid brother Paul came out of the shack. They clustered around him, hugging him and asking a jumble of questions that he didn't even try to sort out. He held onto his mother with one arm and used the other to hug the rest of his family. He smiled at them and spoke softly and gently to his mother, soothing her as best he could. Megan rushed back into the shack and Richard walked his mom up the steps and inside, his father and Paul following. Megan piled up blankets and their two pillows on an army cot to make a sort of chaise longue for her mom and Richard seated her there. But she wouldn't let go of him so he sat beside her, holding her hand.

He looked around to see that there were suit-cases, some open, at one end of the room. Besides the four cots, the only furniture was a single-burner hot plate sitting on top of the potbellied wood stove. The only electrical wiring was a single bulb in the middle of the ceiling. Paul had screwed in an outlet gadget that allowed them to plug in the hot plate as well as operate a light bulb with a pull chain. Megan made tea on the hot plate and brought a cup for her mother.

"I'm sorry, Richard, but there's no sugar or milk or lemon. Would you like a cup of plain tea?"

Richard took the cup from her. "That's okay. I'm sure Mom doesn't mind." He smiled up at Megan then turned to his mother. "Here, Mom, see if you can't drink some tea. It'll do you good."

Gradually, Mrs. Kawashima stopped shaking. When she began to fumble for her handkerchief, Richard took a clean one from his pocket and gave it to her. As she mopped up, he turned to his dad.

"I thought I'd get here the same day you did, but you must have got here yesterday."

Mr. Kawashima nodded. "Yes. We got here just before sunset."

Megan handed her father a cup of tea. He smiled his thanks at her. She sat down on an upended suitcase.

"Luckily," she said, "we didn't have much luggage, just what each of us could carry, so it didn't take long to move in. The government had already furnished the houses – cots and army blankets." She gestured around the room.

Paul spoke up angrily. "This is our living room! This is my bed and that's Megan's. Mom's and Dad's are over there. Only it's daytime now so they're sofas."

"Easy, son." Mr. Kawashima spoke gently. "We must make the best of things."

"We had such a nice house and everything clean and – now this!"

Mrs. Kawashima spoke firmly. "Paul, stop that at once. It's no good lamenting our home and everything – all that's gone. We must make the best of this until the end of the war and then see what we can do."

Paul lapsed into silence but looked as if he were fighting back tears. And no wonder, thought Richard. Yanked out of his security, away from his friends, into a concentration camp. The kid must be scared stiff. He'd adjust, though, and so would Megan. Richard wasn't worried about them, the young rebounded fairly quickly to changed conditions. It was his parents he was worried about, especially his father. He knew his father to be a proud man and this plunging of his family into physical misery and emotional turmoil that he couldn't do anything to alleviate would be plain hell for him.

"Remember Dr. Fujita, Richard, from our old neighborhood?" asked Megan.

"The dentist? Yes, I remember him."

"He's here. I ran into him this morning when I was out looking around. The government is going to let him set up a dental office. He asked me if I would be his assistant."

"What did you say?"

"I told him that I'd talk it over with my family and let him know."

"Good," said Mr. Kawashima. "That's good, Megan, to have work to do." "Yes," agreed Mrs. Kawashima. "If you would like to, I'd say go

253

ahead. Of course, you don't know anything about dentistry."

Megan smiled. "I pointed that out to him. He said it didn't matter, that he would teach me what I need to know."

"What about school?" Richard asked. "Will Paul have a chance to finish high school?"

Mr. Kawashima nodded. "There was an orientation last night in the mess hall. There will be an elementary school and a high school. Teachers will be recruited from among ourselves."

"There's a mess hall, eh?" Richard glanced at the hot plate. "I noticed there was no kitchen here. The meals will be communal, I guess?"

Again Mr. Kawashima answered. "Yes. The women who don't have regular jobs will do the cooking. The men will work in the fields, those who are able-bodied. The older boys, too, after school and on Saturdays."

Paul burst out, "I don't see why we should work for them! We're not farmers. I'd like to kill them all. All these superior white bastards, telling us what to do and where to go."

Mr. Kawashima spoke sharply, imperatively. "Paul! Watch your language."

"Sorry, Father. Sorry, Mother."

Mrs. Kawashima smiled at him. "They're

more to be pitied than blamed, son. Their ignorance is not their fault. They've been made cats' paws by people in authority who really do know better."

Richard looked at his young brother sympathetically. "Mom's right, Paul. But I know how you feel."

Mr. Kawashima looked around at his family and spoke slowly, hoping to impress his words on their minds so that they would never forget. "Right now public opinion is very much against us. Many white Americans disliked us before and now what was done at Pearl Harbor has made every white U.S. citizen feel that killing 'Japs' is a good thing. They do not distinguish between Japanese nationals and Americans of Japanese ancestry. They are not interested in legalities. Interning us is unconstitutional. In spite of Roosevelt's presidential order, it is illegal. But here we are. Now, listen to me very carefully. Paul, Richard, you especially, listen. Be very careful to give no reason for distrust. Be very careful not to inflame the hatred the whites harbor towards us. I have studied white Americans for many years now. I have read of the lynchings in the south when they became enraged with Negroes. I have read of their treatment of Chinese people who looked too prosperous. I have seen the poverty on the Indian reservations in the Dakotas and New Mexico. It takes very little to arouse the racial hatreds of these people to the point of murder. Do nothing to arouse this hatred toward yourself or toward your people. Be circumspect in your speech and in your actions. Be aware that not only your own safety depends on this, but the safety of your mother and sister, your neighbors, your friends. Never forget how vulnerable we all are."

A wave of anger swept through the little room; Richard was shaken with a rage so deep that it startled him with its intensity.

Megan looked at him speculatively. "Why did you come here, Richard? Why didn't you stay clear of the mess in Canada?"

"I was tempted. But I couldn't face myself if I didn't come to share whatever the rest of you had to bear."

"I'm glad you're here," Megan said. "But I think you're a fool."

"An even greater fool than you think, Megan," Richard said softly, thinking of Sheila.

Mrs. Kawashima took his hand in hers again. "There's a girl at last, isn't there?"

Richard laughed. "I've heard that a cold in the head and being in love can't be hid. Yes, Mother mine, there is a girl. What a girl. She has the bluest eyes, the prettiest hair, and the most kissable lips you ever saw. She's a ballerina and right now she's in Victoria, British Columbia."

Paul's lip curled. "You're in love with one of them?"

"Not one of them, Paul. One of us."

"A Japanese with blue eyes?"

There was a slight edge to Richard's voice as he answered. "Did you never notice the color of Mother's eyes?"

"That's different."

"No, it's not. I don't choose to classify people's worth according to the color of their eyes and I don't think you do either, really. Or Mother won't feel welcome in her own family."

"I'm sorry." Paul looked with stricken eyes at his mother. "I'm sorry."

She smiled at him, understanding his unhappiness. "It's all right, Paul. I know this must be the most confusing muddle imaginable to you."

Megan wanted to know more about Richard's girl. "What did you mean when you said she's one of us?"

"She's an American, too. Her name is Sheila and we're engaged. When the war is over, we're going to be married and begin producing babies. She's agreed to a dozen."

Everyone laughed but there was a catch in

Mrs. Kawashima's throat. Her boy was embarking on a very rocky journey and the potential for heartbreak seemed very great to her. He was her first-born but, more than that, he was the tenderest among her children. Where the other two were often thoughtless and demanding, Richard was always careful of her, always considerate of her comfort and peace of mind. But she only squeezed his hand and asked, "A regular dozen or a baker's dozen?"

Richard laughed. "A baker's dozen, of course."

Everyone laughed again.

Mr. Kawashima shared some of his wife's misgivings but had great trust in Richard's native common sense. "Tell us about her. Where she's from and how you met. What her religion is."

"All right. But remember, you asked. Because I could talk about Sheila for hours. For days."

Time seemed to move rapidly. The Kawashima family fell into the rhythm of the camp routine of communal meals, school, and work in the fields. At first there was little restriction on their movements. They were free to leave the camp to shop in the tiny town of Tulelake or even venture into the larger town of Klamath Falls, forty miles up the road and across the state line into Oregon. The Kawashimas were well off and Richard was able to purchase a car and a number of things to make their shack more comfortable.

One thing he couldn't do anything about was the dust and, alternatively, the mud. The soil was fine and light, the bottom of a lake that had been drained twenty years earlier. Even a brisk breeze would set the dust to blowing and it sifted through the cracks of the tarpaper shack, forming drifts under the windows and door. No amount of sweeping and mopping could ever keep the place clean for long. When it rained, it was worse. The thirsty soil soaked up the moisture and instantly turned the streets, unpaved as they were, to bottomless mudholes. Try as they might, they could not scrape it completely off their shoes or keep it out of the house.

Richard and some of the other young men used Sundays to make excursions into the nearby lava beds. Some of them had been to Japan, as had Richard, and knew that those islands were volcanic. Richard sometimes looked at Mt. Shasta and wondered if it could be tied somehow to Mt. Fuji. The thought gave him a sort of uncanny feeling of possible/impossible. He felt that such a connection ought to have profound meaning but could not isolate what the meaning would be.

He learned that the cliff that jutted out into the farmland above the camp was called "The Peninsula" and had, in fact, been a peninsula before the lake was drained. He and his friends explored the area and found a cliff behind The Peninsula that had a frieze of petroglyphs. Strange designs to Richard, full of meaning, no doubt, to those who had carved them. He thought about the time and work it would take to incise those figures into the rock and wondered very much at the people who made them and why it worth such an expenditure to them.

The Modoc Indians, from whom the whites had wrested Tule Lake and the Lava Beds and surrounding hills about seventy years earlier, had called the lava fields and buttes "the land of burnt-out fires." The Modocs had made their last stand in a fortress-like labyrinth of caves and lava rock breastworks. He stood on a boulder at the edge of the stronghold one Sunday afternoon and looked all around. Nothing. There was nothing there that white men could possibly have wanted except some rather poor grazing land. There had been no farm land until the lake had been drained long after the Modocs had fought and lost their war. There were no minerals, no timber.

Richard pondered long on the meaning of the Modoc War. Since the Modocs had nothing that the whites wanted and posed no threat to their safety, why had it been necessary to exterminate them? Because exterminate them, the whites had certainly tried to do. The small remnant of the tribe, which had numbered fewer than a thousand even before the war, had been sent to Oklahoma in the hope that they would intermarry with other Indians and cease to exist as a tribe. He was forced to the conclusion that the whites had destroyed the Modocs simply because they were Indians. Had he known that William Tecumseh Sherman was Commander-in-Chief of the Army during the war, much of his puzzlement would have been cleared up.

The thought of his people at the foot of The Peninsula was too evocative – Richard pushed it away and went to join his buddies who were drinking beer and talking about enlisting in the army. The same army that had sent fifteen hundred soldiers to fight sixty-eight Modocs right there in those rocks. And took more than a year to get the job done.

The townspeople in Tulelake and the other small towns around soon began to object to the internees being allowed to leave the camp almost at will. The farmers, too, claimed to fear for the safety of their families if the "Japs" were allowed to roam free. It wasn't long until guard towers were erected. For the duration of the war, armed soldiers manned the guard towers and patrolled the boundary fences. It became almost impossible to obtain permission to leave the camp except on work details to the fields.

Richard and Paul were assigned to help irrigate the potato fields. This entailed opening the ditches that ran along the end of each field so that the water could run down the rows, soaking the roots of each plant. When the water reached the far end of the row, they shoveled dirt back into the openings to shut the water off. There was no shade in the fields and the work was hot, muddy, and strenuous.

It was not all work and no play. Being Americans, the teenagers and young adults in the camp tuned their radios to the latest song hits. They formed a small band and Richard sang with them at the Saturday night dances in the mess hall. Mrs. Kawashima and some of the other ladies chaperoned the dances and served simple refreshments. If the youngsters noticed the irony in dancing to "Don't Fence Me In," while they were confined in a concentration camp, they made no issue of it.

That fall, Richard spent his days helping with the potato harvest. A digging machine turned the rows so the potatoes were brought to the surface and a crew followed, picking up the spuds and putting them in hundred pound capacity burlap sacks. Each picker wore a heavy leather belt with hooks on the front. Mr. Kawashima was given the job of issuing the sacks, giving each one ten sacks at a time. One was hooked on the front of the belt so that both hands were free to pick up potatoes, and the others on the sides. As each sack was filled half full, the picker unhooked it from his belt and set it on the row. It was hard work, stooping all day long, pulling the sack along until it held fifty pounds, then starting over with an empty sack. At the end of the day Richard could hardly stand up straight. He was so tired at night that he could scarcely eat supper before falling into bed.

The day started as soon as it was light enough for the farmers to see to drive the tractors and pull the diggers through the rows. The pickers stayed in the field as long as necessary to gather all the exposed potatoes so they wouldn't freeze overnight when the temperature dropped. Another crew drove a flat bed truck slowly down the rows to pick up the sacks of potatoes and haul them to the storage cellars.

It was the end of October before the harvest was finished. Two days after, Richard and four of his friends obtained permission to drive into

Klamath Falls to enlist in the army. He returned that night and handed his mother a small service banner with one star on it. Mrs. Kawashima looked from the banner to Richard and began to cry softly. She had known why he went to town that day but the foreknowledge didn't help her much in the face of the reality of his enlistment. He put his arms around her and talked quietly, telling her that he would come home when the war was over and they would begin anew in a new home. Mr. Kawashima sat in one of a pair of armchairs Richard had been able to procure and nodded silently. His son's enlistment was like an arrow in his heart but, at the same time, he was proud of him and felt he was doing the right thing.

Richard put his mother in the other armchair, next to her husband, and took the service banner from her. He hung it on the wall next to the crucifix with its strip of dried palm leaf.

"I'm to report to the train station in Klamath Falls tomorrow," Richard said.

"Where are they sending you?" Mr. Kawashima asked.

Richard grinned at him. "They wouldn't tell us. Afraid we'd send such vital and secret information to the Japanese high command, I guess."

"That's just stupid," Mrs. Kawashima

exclaimed disgustedly.

'I know, Mother. But that's how it is."

"Yes," she sighed. "That's how it is." She took herself in hand and became her usual brisk and sensible self. "Have you told Sheila?"

"I wrote her this afternoon. She understands that I have to go."

"I'll bet she doesn't," retorted Mrs. Kawashima.

"It's enough if she says she does," Mr. Kawashima stated. "In this case, the will to understand suffices."

Mrs. Kawashima shot her husband a skeptical glance. She rose to her feet. "I must get over to the mess hall. I'm on kitchen duty for supper tonight."

Basic training, so strange at first, very quickly felt familiar, even inevitable. Richard's body responded to the relentless exercise and, although he griped like everyone else, he was secretly pleased and looked forward to proving himself in battle. He and the other men in the 442nd regiment were determined to prove themselves as ferocious fighters for Uncle Sam. They suffered many insults, not only from the townspeople when they went in on passes, but from their own drill instructors and even some of their own officers, who were white. But he was their Uncle Sam, too, and every insult strengthened their resolve to acquit themselves superlatively in battle.

Richard and Sheila wrote each other nearly every day. She was touring with the ballet company, criss-crossing the western states and provinces. The travel by train was grueling but the performances were well received and she was enjoying herself, aside from longing to be with him. They planned to spend the time together when Richard got his shipping out leave. Her company would be in Boise, Idaho so they decided to meet in Reno. Richard found himself wanting very intensely to marry her before he went overseas. Then, if he were killed, she would have his G.I. insurance. What stopped him from proposing was what would happen if he were only maimed. He did not want her tied to him if he couldn't take care of her, if she had to take care of him. Sheila hoped that the ease of marriage in Reno would weight the balance scale to her side and their time together would be a honeymoon.

She waited for two days in Reno before she got a telegram from Richard: "Am devastated. Caught mumps. Can't move. Will be lucky ship out with outfit. Writing you Boise. All my love, Richard." There was nothing to do but pack and go back to Boise. An airmail letter awaited her there, explaining everything. She had cried over the telegram and she cried some more over the letter. He loved her and wanted her and wished with all his heart to see her before he shipped overseas but there was not a chance of it. As soon as he could be on his feet again, he would have to report for duty.

Richard raged against his luck the whole time he was in sick bay. He had to do as he was told lest the baker's dozen children become impossible. So he lay in bed and longed for Sheila and cursed the war and the mumps and every circumstance that appeared to be against him. The doctor finally released him from sick bay two days before his outfit shipped out. Those days in bed had cost him some of his hard-won conditioning so he spent a lot of his ship-board time exercising, which wasn't easy under the conditions of the troop ship.

Once he got off the ship, Richard's natural buoyancy allowed him to overcome his depression. By the time they got halfway up Italy, he was a battle-hardened corporal. He hated the war and the dirt and the suffering that was all around him. The 442nd took terrible casualties. They all wanted so fiercely to prove themselves to be just as loyal, just as capable, and just as tough as the white regiments that they threw themselves recklessly into harm's way. They had the highest casualty rate, and the highest medal-winning rate, in the European theatre.

It was raining, had been raining off and on for days. But Richard and his buddies had not been issued slickers or even warm jackets. Thus, Richard stood in his foxhole on the mountainside dressed only in battle fatigues and helmet, eating K rations. He hadn't had a chance to wash or shave for several days and he didn't remember for sure when he'd last had a hot meal. All around him were similar men in similar foxholes. Shell holes pocked the earth all around them. Here and there showed the evidence of shells that had hit their targets.

The enemy artillery was lobbing shells at them from across the valley on another mountain slope. He heard a shell coming in particularly close and ducked down into his foxhole. Gobs of mud splattered down on him and his food. He threw the food away disgustedly and took a drink from his canteen.

Slick, a Nisei from Walla Walla, Washington, glided up to Richard's foxhole.

"Come on, we're moving out."

"Where we goin'?"

"Damned if I know. Up the hill. It's always up the hill."

Richard hoisted himself out of the foxhole and went to help pass the word. They all moved silently up the hill. Presently, they found themselves out of range of the artillery, which continued to pound the position they had just left. They toiled up the mountainside, their numbers increasing as they went and other soldiers joined them. Towards dark, as they were about to bivouac, Richard pointed out a barn that still had most of its roof intact. He and six or eight of his buddies reconnoitered but found nothing ominous. Inside the barn was a large pile of hay.

Richard smiled with satisfaction. "We'll sleep warm tonight, boys."

"First time in a week," Tet remarked.

"Nine days," corrected Richard.

They burrowed into the hay, trading the discomfort of hay in their clothing and down their necks for the comfort of warmth. Richard woke the next morning to find a hen clucking contentedly in front of his face. She was scratching busily in the hay and pecking the seeds she loosened. Slowly, cautiously, he reached out one hand and grabbed her by the legs. She squawked and flapped her wings but he held on while he extricated himself from the hay. Once on his feet, he quickly wrung her neck. The others were delighted. While Richard picked the hen, Tet and Slick brought a couple of pots of water to boil over a small fire.

"Hot coffee, fresh meat, and a warm bed," Richard sighed. "If I was clean, I'd think I'd died and gone to heaven."

Leon came out from a corner of the barn just then, holding his helmet upside-down.

"Clean or not," he said, "I believe we have died and gone to heaven. Look here, what I've got."

They gathered around and looked.

"Eggs!" Slick was incredulous. "I don't believe it. Great day in the morning, eggs."

"Wait a minute," Tet cautioned, "before you go to rhapsodizing. They may be eggs or they may be chickens. You city boys are all alike. Don't know where milk comes from; think vegetables grow in tin cans. If that hen has been setting on those eggs long, they'll be past the white and yolk stage and into the chick stage."

Richard sat back down and resumed his picking. "Well, break one open and see."

"*Waste* one?" demanded Slick.

"Nah. We'll candle 'em," Tet said. "Here, Leon, let me have 'em."

Suspiciously, Leon handed the helmet to Tet, who sat down in front of the fire and took a pot of water off. He held up an egg in front of the flame.

270

"They're okay," he announced. "Let's boil 'em."

"Wait a minute," said Leon. "I ain't getting' my face all fixed for boiled eggs and find out only one of 'em's good. Do the rest."

"There's only one hen," Tet protested. "The eggs are all about the same age. That means if one's good, they're all good. Eggs in the same nest all hatch the same day."

"Leon's right," Slick said. "Go ahead, Tet, candle all of 'em."

Tet sighed and candled all the eggs.

After breakfast, they heated more water for washing and shaving. Some strolled outside, some lit cigarettes and lounged in the barn. Richard was shaving when Slick stuck his head in the door.

"Hey, you guys, mail call!"

"Where?" Richard barked.

"Jeep's about a hundred yards up the hill."

Richard hurriedly finished shaving and followed the others outside. A corporal was pulling letters and parcels out of a mail bag and calling the names of the addressees. The men listened eagerly and grabbed happily when their names were called. Richard took his two letters back to the barn and sat on the floor to read them. He read the one from his mother and smiled as he folded it and put it in his pocket. The family was fine; Paul had promised to finish high school before he enlisted. He opened Sheila's letter and read it with growing excitement. Tet looked over at him.

"Looks like you got some good news," he said.

"It's Sheila," Richard said. "She's joined a USO show – I told you that."

Tet grinned. "Seems like I remember hearing something about it."

Richard grinned back. "Never mind that. She's coming to Italy."

"When? Where in Italy?"

"She'll be in Bergamo next week. After that she'll be playing all over the country."

"You gonna get married?"

Richard nodded happily. "I told her in my last letter that I have the right papers for it and she says that's what she's coming for."

"You lucky dog."

"Yeah. Now all I have to do is wangle some way to get to Bergamo."

Richard didn't have much problem wangling a pass to Bergamo. His immediate superiors knew all about Sheila and sympathized with the young couple. So he was on the landing field in his class A uniform when her plane touched down. The plane taxied up close to the hangar and the ground crew rolled the steps up to the door. Six women, all dressed in WAC uniforms, came down the steps. Sheila ran to Richard and threw herself into his arms. They embraced and kissed, holding one another frantically, as if afraid the other would vanish as in so many dreams. The woman who was shepherding the girls came over to them and Sheila introduced them.

"Richard, this is Mrs. Leibkowicse. Lucille, Richard Kawashima. Lucille's our road manager."

Lucille nodded shortly. "Corporal. Glad to meet you. Sheila, you and your friend will have some time together later. Right now we have to get checked into the hotel."

Sheila laughed. "Oh, Lucille, I'm not going to waste Richard's three-day pass on checking into hotels. The first show is tomorrow at the hospital here in Bergamo. I'll be there in plenty of time. And Richard'll sing for you, too."

"Sheila, I'm responsible for you while…"

Richard interrupted, his arm around Sheila's waist. "Come now, Lucille," he said with a charming smile. "Think how you'd feel if you were in love and had been separated for a long time and just got reunited with your lover and some old battleaxe tried to separate you again."

Mrs. Leibkowicse drew herself up and jutted out her chin but Richard didn't give her a chance to speak.

273

"There," he said, "I knew you wouldn't want to be an old battleaxe. We're going to get married now and we'll see you tomorrow. Tell the band to rehearse 'Pistol Packin' Mama' because I'm going to sing it with them."

Before Lucille had recovered from all that, Richard and Sheila grabbed her suitcases where the ground crew had set them and walked across the tarmac. Sheila waved at the other girls, who called good wishes after them.

They took a rattletrap taxi to the small hotel where Richard had taken a room. Once inside, Richard dropped the suitcases and folded Sheila in his arms. They stood in the middle of the room and kissed.

"I can't believe you're really here," Richard murmured.

"Neither can I. Oh, Richard, it's been such a long time."

"It won't be much longer, though, before we can forget all this and be together always." He released her and she went to the mirror over the dresser and took off her hat. Richard sat on the edge of the bed and watched as she smoothed her hair. "We have this winter to slog it out through the rest of Italy and then France but everyone knows Germany is on her last legs. I'll be home for good next summer."

Sheila turned a radiant face to him. "Just think of it – our own home. Just the two of us. Until we get started on producing all those babies."

She crossed the room to stand in front of him. He pulled her down beside him and crushed her to him, kissing her eyes, her lips, her cheeks, her hair. She clung to him, half-laughing, half-crying, repeating his name over and over. Suddenly, he sat up and let go of her.

"Sheila. First things first," he said urgently. "Do you intend to be married in that uniform?"

"No, of course not. I've brought the most heavenly wedding dress. At least, it isn't exactly a wedding dress. But it's white and has a matching hat with a little veil. Wait till you see it."

"Put it on, quickly."

Reluctantly, with a lingering kiss, she stood up and looked around for her suitcases.

"Which bag is it in?" Richard asked.

She pointed. "That one."

He put it on a chair for her and opened it. Then he sat on the bed with his back against the headboard and watched as she took a lovely cream silk brocade suit out. She held it up to show him.

"Very nice," he said appreciatively.

Sheila shot him a smile and took off her uniform. She twisted to see if her stocking seams were straight. As she stepped out of her uniform

275

shoes, she noticed that Richard seemed to be in some sort of discomfort; he was squirming a bit, as if his uniform had become too tight. The reason dawned on her.

"Oh, I'm sorry. Shall I go into the bathroom?"

"The bathroom is down the hall. No, it's okay, I like it. Only, don't take too long."

She smiled at him and attended to her makeup and hair. She put the suit on and a little cream lace hat with a cluster of pink roses on one side of it. She slipped on satin pumps and turned to him.

"I'm ready, Richard."

"So am I."

Sheila started toward him and he hastily got off the bed and opened the door. As they walked to the church, children accosted them, begging. Richard gave them coins. An elderly woman stood near the fountain in the center of the square with flowers to sell. Richard bought a nosegay of pink roses. Sheila solemnly detached one of the roses and pinned it to his uniform lapel. They kissed and didn't notice the silent tears that rolled down the old woman's cheeks.

Luckily, the priest they found at the church spoke some English. Richard and Sheila had both taken Latin in school and been trained to understand Mass and the other church ceremonies that were all conducted in Latin, but they didn't find it much help in speaking or understanding idiomatic Italian. The priest studied the paper that Richard handed him.

"This way, please," he said at length.

"Thank you, Father," Richard said, as he and Sheila followed. He smiled at his bride. She squeezed his arm and smiled back at him.

The ceremony was short but they both knew, as Richard slipped the little golden band on her finger, that it would remain one of their most precious memories in the years to come. The priest pronounced them man and wife and stood beaming at them as they kissed. Richard gave him a wad of lira and he and Sheila shook hands with him.

Their hearts were bursting with happiness as they came out of the church, their hands entwined. Once more they were accosted by begging children. Richard gave them coins but one tiny, big-eyed girl caught at his heart. He squatted to talk to her. Several other children stood alertly behind her, watching his smallest gesture, hopeful yet wary.

"Are you hungry, bambina?" he asked softly. She merely looked at him unblinkingly. He rubbed his stomach. "Fame?" he asked in Italian. All the children nodded, half-hopefully, half-suspiciously. "Come," he said, "we'll eat." They appeared not to understand so he repeated it in Italian. "Venire. Mangiare."

A small boy perked up. "Mangiare?"

Sheila smiled at him. "Yes. Si. Mangiare."

Richard and Sheila shepherded the children into a nearby restaurant. They all sat at a big round table and the proprietor came to wait on them. He looked rather alarming to Sheila with his big black mustache and his piercing brown eyes.

"Do you speak English, signore?" asked Richard.

"Si, a little English I speak," he said. His English was heavily accented but Richard could make out his meaning.

"This is our wedding supper," he explained, "so we want the best you have to offer."

"Your wedding day." The proprietor smiled at Sheila. "My felicitations to you both. These are the wedding guests, no doubt," he added, with a sweeping gesture at the children.

"These are our children," Sheila told him. "For tonight. We are trying it out, to see if we'd like a large family."

"A very good idea, signora."

"What is the specialty of your house?" Richard asked.

"Rigatoni with bread and wine. A rich, red wine. Chianti."

"Bring us, if you please, the pasta and the bread," Richard ordered. "But not the wine. We're already drunk with happiness, you understand. Bring milk."

The proprietor nodded and disappeared into the kitchen. The children watched Richard and Sheila warily but with growing confidence. There was a battered old upright piano against the wall and while they were waiting, Richard and Sheila went to it. Sheila sat at the keyboard and Richard stood beside her.

Sheila grinned up at him. "What'll it be, soldier?"

Richard began to croon, "Night and day, you are the one, only you, beneath the moon and under the sun." He looked into her eyes then shook himself, changing his mood. "We need something to entertain our guests. Do you know 'Elmer's Tune'?"

"Sure."

Sheila played it and Richard sang. He danced around the children, singing and mugging for them to their great delight. The proprietor made several trips from the kitchen, bringing dishes and flatware, bread and milk. The children snatched at the bread and ate as they watched Richard. But he lost his audience completely when the big bowl of rigatoni appeared. The children had eyes for nothing but the food. Richard and Sheila took their places at the table. They crossed themselves and the children did likewise. They all bowed their heads. Richard said grace. "Thank you, o Lord, in these Thy gifts which we are about to receive through the bounty of Christ our Lord. Amen."

Sheila passed the plates to Richard; he filled them and she passed them to the children. It gave the two of them a great deal of satisfaction to fill the children full of wholesome food but they knew that months, maybe years, of deprivation lay ahead for them.

When they got back to their hotel and stood in the corridor outside their door, Richard unlocked it. Then he turned and swung Sheila up into his arms. He carried her over the threshold and they kissed. He kicked the door shut behind him and Sheila slid to her feet, down the length of his body. His breath was coming quickly as he reached behind him to lock the door.

"I have a gorgeous negligee," she murmured. "I'll put it on for you."

He removed her hat and put it on the dresser. He took the nosegay from her and put it carefully beside the hat.

"My passion needs no titillation tonight," he breathed, and began to unbutton her suit jacket.

The next afternoon Sheila and Richard joined the troupe at an open air stage to perform for the G.I.s. The wounded men were in the front rows with the others seeming a veritable sea of faces. Mrs. Leibkowicse acted as mistress of ceremonies. A small band played and the girls danced, wearing short skirts and high heels that elicited much whistling and applause from the audience. As the final number of the set ended, Richard ran out onto the stage, took Sheila by the hand and leaned down to ask the band to play another song. He was wearing his uniform so every man in the audience identified with him. They danced a very fancy jitterbug and Richard finished it by taking Sheila into a deep backbend and kissing her. The audience cheered.

Mrs. Leibkowicse came out on stage and announced into the microphone, waving a hand at Richard and Sheila, "Mr. and Mrs. Richard Kawashima. They were married yesterday."

The audience cheered again and called out felicitations and advice.

Mrs. Leibkowicse continued, "I don't know what this war is coming to. Can't even bring the girls for you guys to look at without you run off and marry 'em."

The audience laughed delightedly.

"Well, anyhow," Mrs. Leibkowicse added,

"Richard's done a little singing before the war and he'd like to keep his voice in shape so he can go to Hollywood and be a star. Sing it for us, Richard."

She stepped back from the mike and joined the applause as Richard stepped up to it, keeping a tight hold on Sheila. First he sang a couple of popular novelty songs, then he sang a sweet and sentimental love song, his arm around Sheila's waist. The audience grew very quiet and remained quiet for a moment after the song ended. Then the applause began and went on and on.

The next day the show was scheduled for a little camp out in the mountains. Richard and Sheila were in the back of a Jeep; Mrs. Leibkowicse was up in front with the soldier driver. There was very little traffic on the dirt road. Up ahead, well out of range, they could see an artillery duel.

"Poor bastards," Richard said. "They're sure getting the hell pounded out of 'em. I hope the dogfaces have been pulled out."

Sheila looked at him in surprised consternation. "My God. Don't tell me there are men on that hillside where the shells are falling."

"I hope not," he answered.

"Have you ever been under that kind of fire?" she asked.

"Yes, of course. It's one of the things that soldiers are for." Richard squeezed her hand. "Don't worry, Sweetheart. I'm going to come out all right. We're going to have our dozen kids."

The noise of the artillery had masked the sound of some planes coming up behind them. When he finally heard them, Richard looked up and back, expecting to see a flight of allied planes. He had just time to note the Nazi insignia before the strafing started.

Sheila was smiling at him. "Our baker's dozen."

The bullets cut a double path up the road and through all four of the people in the Jeep.

Epilogue

Pat was still in trance, lying back in Dr. Parker's recliner. He looked very puzzled. "I don't know what's happened. I don't see Sheila. I don't even see the Jeep."

Dr. Parker leaned forward. "Has there been an accident?"

"I don't...Oh. Oh, I see. That German plane strafed us. The Jeep is on its side in the ditch. The soldier and Mrs. Leibkowicse are dead. Sheila's dead, too."

"And you, Pat?"

"Yes, I'm dead. But not really. Our bodies are lying there beside the Jeep but we're still alive." Pat raised his head and looked away from Dr. Parker, as if listening. "What? Yes, Darling. It's the fourth dimension or somewhere like that."

"Who are you talking to, Pat?"

"Sheila. She's confused. She wanted to know if we were dead and in heaven. I must go to her."

Dr. Parker waited a few moments then began to bring Pat out of his hypnotic trance. She instructed him to remember what he'd seen and done while hypnotized.

'Starla was very angry, Doctor," he explained. "She thought we were cheated and I agree. We had the world in front of us – the whole of our lives. It's not fair to have it all taken from us like that."

"You didn't feel like that about any of the other lives you've told me about, did you?"

"None of them were the same situation. I was angry that Starla just gave up there in the Caribbean when we were so close to making it. But, as it turned out, it was best. There was really no future for us there."

"You weren't angry at the way you died in Atlantis."

"When she murdered me? No, I wasn't angry with her. I didn't understand about the Things. And about her daughter. It was necessary that I should die to give her daughter a chance in that life. I'm just glad I had a chance to make it up to her."

"Does she feel remorse that she killed you?"

"No. It was necessary. Oh, she felt badly while she was in flesh in that life. But she was more angry than remorseful. Angry that I was so unreasonable that she had to do it."

"Did you incur karmic debt because of your granddaughter?"

"Yes. I paid for it, though. I lost my children in the next life. Because of what I tried to do to my granddaughter, my wives and children were taken from me. And then, when I'd found Starla again, she left me. I was angry with her about that. And Starla was angry with me for suiciding."

"Is that why you had no children in the Caribbean life?"

"Yes. We weren't ready yet. And in the Indian life I was only allowed one child. Starla was my son in that life. Did you realize that?"

"No, I didn't."

"It's time I was allowed a family again. Starla and I discussed it. We decided to incarnate again as soon as possible and to live into old age surrounded by ten children and dozens of grand-children."

Dr. Parker made a note on her pad. "When you use expressions like 'I've paid,' do you mean that in order to punish you for past transgressions, God has set certain conditions in your lives? That it's all pre-ordained?"

"No, of course not. He gives us additional opportunities. In order to learn a needed lesson, certain conditions are necessary."

"So He doesn't punish the innocent along with the guilty?"

"Never. For instance, in the African life my wives and children all had their own karmic reasons for being there and for dying as they did."

"Why was it necessary for the pirate captain to enslave you?"

"Because I'd held the Things in bondage and been cruel to them. And because I'd enslaved

287

Starla. It was necessary for me to learn at first hand the cruelties of bondage."

"Yet it seemed an enjoyable captivity."

Pat frowned thoughtfully. "In a way. The captain was a very sexy lady. But not every man is psychologically suited to the role of gigolo. I wasn't. Actually, I could have escaped fairly easily. My mind and emotions were enslaved, not my body. Or maybe it would be more accurate to say that my mind and emotions were enslaved by my body. I don't know. It's very simple and, at the same time, very complex."

"Will you and Starla be able to work out your differences now so you can be happy together?"

"I think so. I'm not sure because we incarnated again too soon. We didn't take enough time to process the last life. And the confusion and turmoil of the world are so accessible, it's hard to shut it out so we can concentrate on ourselves. It really makes me angry that we had worked out an equilibrium and had everything in place to live as we wanted last time and then to have it all taken away from us like that."

"Maybe that anger is what's between you and happiness with Starla this time."

"That's very astute, Doctor. Especially since Starla's angry, too. But maybe now that I know the source of the anger, we can come to some kind of truce with it. At least she's talking to me again. I have a date with her tonight."

"Does she know about your sessions here?"

Pat smiled. "She knows I've been seeing a shrink. She doesn't know about the reincarnation bit. I'm going to broach the subject tonight."

"Well, Pat, if I can be of any further help, don't hesitate to call me. And do let me know how things work out with Starla, will you?"

Pat nodded and went to the door. He turned with his hand on the knob. "Sure thing. Oh, by the way, it seems you and I have some unfinished business."

Dr. Parker was surprised. "How's that?"

"Well, you were Riavay. And Mbonimana. And Hezekiah. And the Pirate Captain."

Her jaw dropped and she stared at him, trying to comprehend all that his words implied. Pat grinned and winked and went out the door.

That evening Starla and Pat met at a very plush restaurant in Scottsdale. It was formal in an Arizonian kind of way so Pat wore very dark blue slacks with a dark iridescent shirt. Starla wore a gown of purple taffeta, severely plain in its lines but giving the effect of lush sensuality. They sat in a high-backed semi-circular banquette that gave them the illusion of privacy. Tall flutes of champagne stood in front of them and they sipped as they talked.

"Pat, I've been exploring something and I want to tell you about it but I'm sort of afraid to."

"Afraid to? Why?"

"Well, I don't want you to think I'm crazy."

Pat put his hand over hers and smiled at her. "After the way I've been spending my Thursday afternoons, I don't think I'd better label anyone."

"All right." Starla took a deep breath. "All right. I've been seeing a hypnotist and he's been regressing me. To past lives, you know."

Pat began to laugh and Starla pulled her hand away from his.

"Don't be offended, Starla." He smiled engagingly and she let him re-capture her hand. "I'm only laughing because that's what I've been doing."

"You've been regressing to past lives, too?"

Pat nodded, still smiling.

"Atlantis?" she asked.

"Yes. Africa? The Caribbean? Absoroka?"

Starla nodded. "The Pirate Captain. I wonder what the Pirate Captain is doing these days."

Pat laughed again. "Oh, Starla. She's my shrink."

Starla shot him an incredulous look and saw that in spite of his laughter, he was perfectly serious. Then she began to laugh with him.

About the Author

Barbara J. Olexer, a fourth-generation Oregonian, has written more than twenty books and screenplays. Her formative years were spent in small farming towns and a backwoods logging camp. Barbara's life has been a tapestry of changes as she has lived and worked in small towns and some of the country's biggest cities. She has retired and returned to the Pacific Northwest, where her children and grandchildren also live. Her home is in Milwaukie, Oregon.